VICTORIA

FALLS

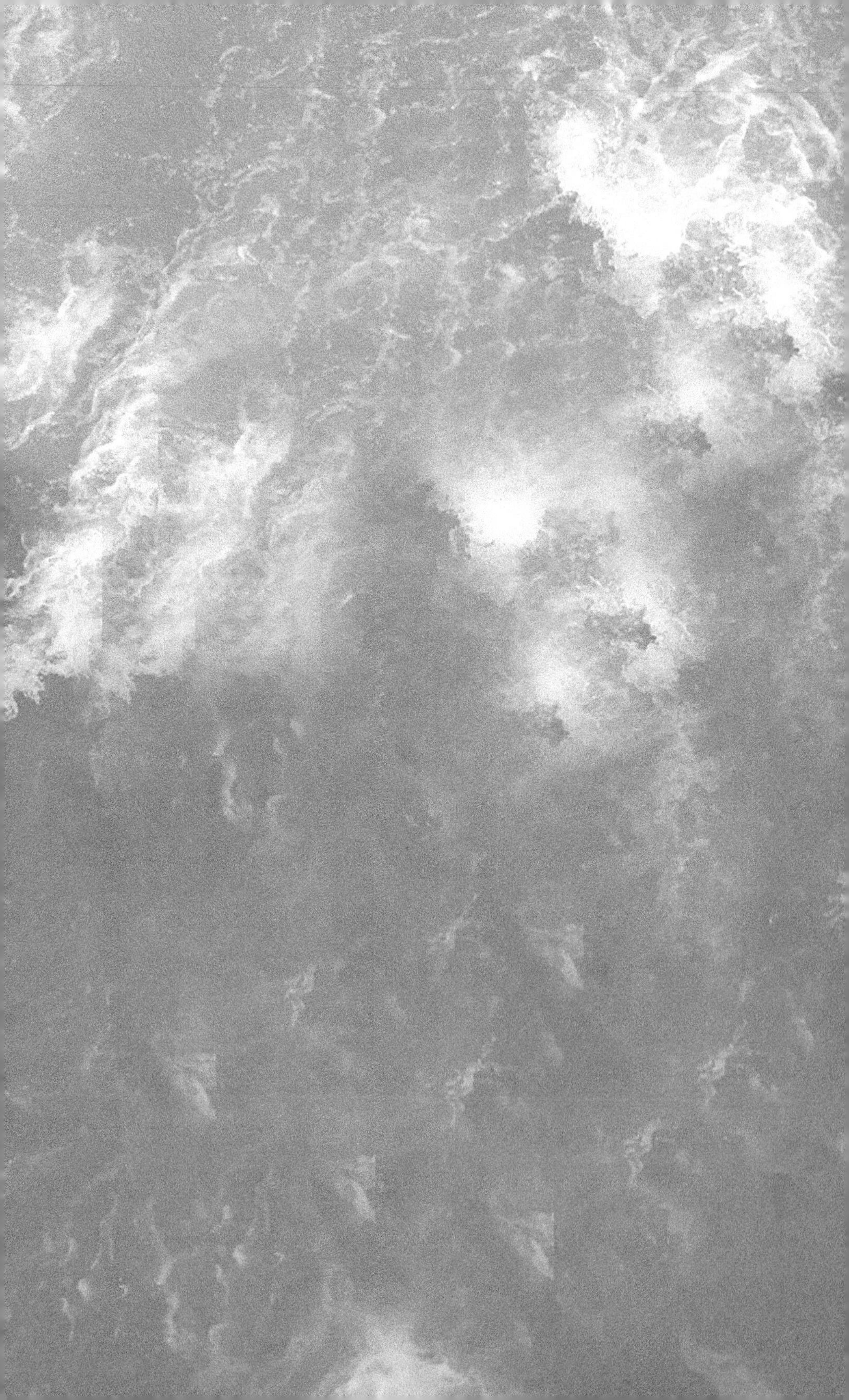

VICTORIA FALLS

A NOVEL

JAMES HORNOR

GREEN PLACE BOOKS | *Brattleboro, Vermont*

Printed in the United States

10 9 8 7 6 5 4 3 2 1

Victoria Falls is a work of fiction. Apart from the actual historic figures, events, and locales that provide background for the narrative, all names, characters, places, and incidents are products of the author's imagination or are used fictitiously.

Green Writers Press is a Vermont-based publisher whose mission is to spread a message of hope and renewal through the words and images we publish. Throughout we will adhere to our commitment to preserving and protecting the natural resources of the earth. To that end, a percentage of our proceeds will be donated to environmental activist groupsand The Southern Poverty Law Foundation. Green Writers Press gratefully acknowledges support from individual donors, friends, and readers to help support the environment and our publishing initiative. Green Place Books curates books that tell literary and compelling stories with a focus on writing about place—these books are more personal stories/memoir and biographies.

Giving Voice to Writers & Artists Who Will Make the World a Better Place
Green Writers Press | Brattleboro, Vermont
www.greenwriterspress.com

ISBN: 978-0-9990766-9-9

PRINTED ON PAPER WITH PULP THAT COMES FROM FSC-CERTIFIED FORESTS, MANAGED FORESTS THAT GUARANTEE RESPONSIBLE ENVIRONMENTAL, SOCIAL, AND ECONOMIC PRACTICES BY LIGHTNING SOURCE. ALL WOOD PRODUCT COMPONENTS USED IN BLACK AND WHITE, STANDARD COLOR OR SELECT COLOR PAPERBACK BOOKS, UTILIZING EITHER CREAM OR WHITE BOOKBLOCK PAPER, THAT ARE MANUFACTURED IN THE LAVERGNE, TENNESSEE PRODUCTION CENTER ARE SUSTAINABLE FORESTRY INITIATIVE (SFI) CERTIFIED SOURCING.

The fear of the Lord is the beginning of wisdom.

—Proverbs 1:7

Bless you prison, bless you for being in my life. For there, lying upon the rotting prison straw, I came to realize that the object of life is not prosperity as we are made to believe, but the maturity of the human soul.

—Aleksander Solzhenitsyn, *The Gulag Archipelago, 1918–1956*

For Eileen

CHAPTER ONE

Flying in a plane without a pressurized cabin makes you more aware of the altitude. I could tell that Sheldon, our former RAF pilot, flew in the same way that professional racers drive—he listened to the engine, ignoring most of the instrument panel in favor of pilot instinct. These twice-a-day forays over the thunderous roar of Victoria Falls were the last vestige of his earlier life as a Royal Air Force war pilot, reaffirming his remarkable agility with the joystick and providing the intoxicating sense of freedom, albeit momentary, he must have experienced flying his Supermarine Spitfire over the fields of France at night, the steady hum of the engine the only link to the safety and civilization he had left behind.

The falls themselves present a full array of challenges to a single-engine plane. Depending on the season, there is fog and mist to contend with along with constant plumes of spray. If your dive below the crest of the falls is at too steep an angle, the plane can stall as it lifts out of the gorge. If the dive is too shallow, you risk crashing into the high embankments on the Zambia side and falling headlong into the gorge. For a conservative pilot, neither of these possibilities would ever materialize; for Sheldon, the exhilaration of cheating death was a daily occurrence.

As the plane dipped and rolled over the vast expanse of falls, Teresa Benjamin instinctively grabbed my hand.

"Crocodiles!" Sheldon yelled back at us, and he half pointed to the banks of the Zambezi on the Zambia side, which somehow seemed above us as we crested over the lip of the falls. Several crocodiles lay basking on the riverbank, seemingly oblivious to the vertical drop just a few meters away.

"You should join us for cocktails."

Our hands were now pressed together, and we were banking back over the falls and directly into a rainbow created by the mountains of spray.

Teresa Benjamin, as I was later to discover, was completely fearless, and her invitation for cocktails as we followed the rush of water over the falls was also an early indication of her constant delight in magnifying the intensity of any emotionally charged moment by transforming it into something of her own creation.

"Do you mean this evening?" I shouted back, feigning the same nonchalance and realizing that I had just missed the opportunity to speak directly into her ear.

"We'll meet you at six."

I sensed that I had earned at least temporary acceptance with her and that it would never have happened this way in any other context. As if to confirm that intuition, Sheldon chose as his finale to fly under Victoria Falls Bridge—certainly not a part of his normal itinerary, yet a stunt (I hoped) he'd performed on earlier occasions.

"I've never hit a bungee jumper yet," he shouted as we roared through.

Teresa smiled broadly as he confidently pulled back on the rudder and we lifted, birdlike, out of the gorge. As we rumbled to a stop on the grass runway above the falls, Teresa placed her right hand on Sheldon's right shoulder.

"Nice piece of flying." She emphasized "nice" in a way that sort of rolled off her tongue. I realized at that moment that the few additional risks he had taken were all for her. Some men can't resist taking it to the limit when there is a woman involved. I thought of those Hemingway short stories where the guide ends up sleeping with the wife of an insipid husband.

She turned; in fact, she deftly pivoted in the confined cockpit, lightly touched my face, and was halfway across the field before I realized that I was still seated, my seatbelt still buckled, simply staring back at her as she strolled toward the hotel.

"Wanna go up again?"

"No," I replied, "One Flight of Angels is probably enough for one day."

At dinner that evening I was reminded of all the reasons I love sub-Saharan Africa. While I was only there on an eight-week mission as an AFREA consultant to the World Bank, on previous assignments in Africa for the Bank and earlier for the IMF, I had come to appreciate the incredible drama of the African landscape. It has the illusion of always being in motion, and indeed the constant movement of exotic wildlife is accentuated by the light that is at once muted, and at the same time vibrant, creating an affinity of existence that can only be described as prelapsarian.

In the late afternoons in Zimbabwe, a russet-colored light blankets the land and the sky in a splendid surrender to the day. The entire subcontinent begins to settle in for the night and the air has a velvety texture that is both soothing and strangely exhilarating.

I arrived for cocktails promptly at six and found the Benjamins enjoying a drink on the outdoor veranda of The Victoria Falls Hotel. The hotel was built in 1906, just five years after the end of Queen Victoria's sixty-three-year reign. It remains one of those extant outposts of British imperialism, and despite Zimbabwe's political independence in 1980, there are vestiges of British influence throughout what had been Southern Rhodesia.

Despite all of our non-proliferation treaties, many Americans like at least the idea of empire, even if it is more a romantic notion than a political reality. It is always interesting to watch Americans on holiday in one of these post-empire (yet nevertheless very British) settings, since American parents somehow expect their children to behave in a manner that they perceive to be more British, and so more "proper," and adults do the same.

"James, I don't think you've met my husband, Richard."

"My pleasure."

"Delighted."

Suddenly we were both addressing one another like Eton school chums.

"Teresa tells me you had quite a flight over the falls."

I immediately thought of Teresa's elegant fingers as she had taken my hand into hers as the plane crested above the Zambezi.

"We had a flight that certainly deserves a stiff drink." Now I was sounding stilted and faux British. "What brings you to Africa?" I was aware that it was not a question I would normally ask in America but somehow in this setting it didn't sound so ridiculous.

"It was actually Teresa's idea. She made me promise that we would go on safari before she turned forty, so we only have two years to spare." Teresa had been attended to by several hotel waiters, and now she walked toward us and gave me one of her broad smiles.

"What are you drinking, James?"

Her white cotton dress reflected the intoxicating glow of the African sunset so that it seemed as if she had lived her entire life on this veranda.

"You should try their gimlets. The bartender is from Cambridge, so he knows how to mix cocktails for academics."

"Do I appear to be an academic?"

"You appear to be studious, which is the same thing."

Teresa moved very close to me, allowing her hair to brush lightly across my shoulder.

"Mr. Monroe works for the World Bank," interjected Richard, and I wondered how much more he knew about my sojourn in Zimbabwe.

"I do research for the Bank," which was only partly true since my work did involve limited research. I sensed that Teresa actually hoped that I really was a quiet and introspective academic.

"Are you related to President James Monroe?" Teresa was now standing between Richard and me, holding her gimlet glass as if she actually owned the hotel, which immediately alerted me to the fact that Richard probably had little in the way of ancestral heritage.

"President Monroe's brother, Andrew Augustine Monroe, was five generations back on my father's side. They were all from Westmoreland County, Virginia. My family is from Fredericksburg, and there are at least five Monroes—including President Monroe—who attended William and Mary. I was the renegade. Against my father's wishes I went to Washington and Lee."

Teresa seemed genuinely interested, but Richard had turned away and was striding across the terrace with children in tow.

"Escort me into dinner, James." I felt her arm slip through mine with the same graceful confidence I noticed as she exited the airplane.

"Tell me more about Virginia and the research you do for the World Bank."

I lay there under the plume of mosquito netting, the low roar of the falls in the distance. Since my divorce I sought out these moments where I reached an equilibrium—a temporary satisfaction when all the disparate parts of my existence seemed to coalesce due to a harmony of circumstance. Victoria Falls, where the unsuspecting Zambezi is flung headlong into the abyss, seemed a great equalizer. A place of terror and authority, where man tempted fate with airplane antics and bungee jumps. A place of endless fascination, where people stand for hours just observing. The circumstance of the falls and all the unlikely events of the previous day reinforced my anonymity, the quiet mystery that I longed to envelop my existence. I would probably never see Teresa and Richard Benjamin again, and yet there we were enjoying cocktails and dinner together on the veranda. We could have been neighbors with adjoining lawns in Lake Forest. Yet I preferred that these brief forays into normalcy ended without expectation, without further commitment.

I awakened a little after two to the sound of voices probably twenty yards from my window. The constant din of the falls made it hard to make out what was being said. I went to the window. Out past the veranda, near the path leading down to the falls, were two people, a man and a woman, arguing. They shouted at intervals, and one of the voices sounded like Teresa's. I stood there for a quarter of an hour as their voices fluctuated from barely audible to occasional exclamations or shouts.

A few minutes later the man—it was clearly Richard Benjamin—came walking back up the hill alone and disappeared into the hotel. I gazed into the darkness, thinking that Teresa would also soon return, but thirty minutes passed with no sign of her.

I thought about going back to bed. Their marital conflicts—no matter how serious—really did not involve me. Teresa and I were barely more than acquaintances, although I thought of her lovely fingers in mine just twelve hours earlier and the way she had lightly touched my face as she exited the plane.

For several minutes I was frozen by indecision, gazing blankly into the darkness. Finally, I hastily dressed and headed out of the hotel across the veranda and down to the path that led to the falls.

If this had been the United States, there would have been security gates and permanent lighting on a path leading to falls that were twice as high as Niagara. But, this was sub-Saharan

Africa, and because of the overhanging trees, the path was close to pitch black. Using the railing, I began the long descent, now vaguely aware that the local wildlife (including the monkeys and baboons that Sheldon had mentioned) were as unregulated as the path itself.

The navigation of the path became even more of a challenge once I came to the section that was continually inundated with spray from the falls, the lights of the hotel quickly retreating behind me. I was suddenly reminded of the spelunking adventure of a decade earlier with my daughter, Jenny. She was only nine or ten at the time and we were exploring a cave in southern West Virginia.

The section of the cave we were in had an underground stream that led into a narrow gorge. The small path came to a point where only one person at a time could slip through the crevice into the next cavern. The cave was lit with a primitive electric system that was reminiscent of pictures of underground coal mines in the 1930s. Jenny was ahead of me on the path and had just slipped through the narrow crevice when all the lights first went dim, then completely out. It was pitch black. I couldn't even see my hands.

"Jenny, can you hear me?"

"I can hear you, Dad." Her voice sounded surprisingly far away.

"Just stay where you are, I will come to you."

Whatever she said next I couldn't really understand.

"Stay right there, sweetie. I will come for you."

And I began to crawl down the path on all fours, feeling with my hands the delineation of the rocks lining the narrow passage. Just before I reached her, the lights flickered and came back on. But in the ten-minute interval of complete blackness, it was just our two voices connecting—father and daughter drawn back together after five years of separation.

"I will come for you."

It was the secret wish of all children of divorced parents—that they would not be abandoned, that all the love and trust from early childhood was real, that their connection, even engulfed in darkness, was mysteriously sustained by the reassuring sound of their parents' voice.

I struggled down the pitch-black walkway, now only vaguely aware of the hotel one hundred yards up the hill. I knew that the Zambezi River was far below, and in the complete darkness I began to imagine that if I slipped and fell forward, there would be little resistance to my body rolling down the steep embankment and into the river. This imagined fear was intensified by the sound of the falls and the continuous clouds of spray that saturated the walkway and soaked my white cotton shirt and chinos.

Through the darkness I saw a dim outline of a figure down and to my left. She was standing, facing the falls on a small platform that extended ten feet from the walkway. Although her back was turned, as I moved slowly down the walkway, I could see that she was crying and her hair was already wet from the spray as she attempted to tuck a small strand behind her left ear. We were now both soaked with spray, which in the darkness seemed to accentuate the complete loneliness of the situation, and I suddenly realized how ridiculous it would be for me to approach her on the small platform. She was a married woman who had been fighting with her husband. Her escape down the walkway had simply been a way for her to separate from him for a short while before returning to the hotel and to her marriage. I wanted to avoid attachments, but perhaps I was unwilling to accept the abject loneliness which seemed now to engulf me in indecision.

At that very moment she turned with arms crossed and began to walk back towards the pathway. I could have avoided her altogether if at the same moment I too had turned and started back towards the hotel. Instead I froze, seemingly incapable of forming any response to her shadowy figure as she made her way up the walkway.

"Teresa, it's me."

It was one of those moments when the sound of your own

voice sounds foreign and unattached to anything. Now she was frozen and not moving.

"James?"

I struggled to decipher her intonation of my name, searching in that split second for some shred of reassurance that she was somehow glad to see me.

"What the hell are you doing down here?"

And in that three or four seconds she had brought back the Teresa from the airplane, the cocktails Teresa from the terrace. She had moved quickly from the unguarded Teresa (perhaps even vulnerable Teresa) to the persona who confronted all situations—even her marriage—with casual fearlessness.

"I couldn't sleep. I heard voices on the terrace, and I saw you from the window as you headed for the walkway."

It sounded contrived, but Teresa had assumed a certain trust towards me that was evident even on the airplane. It was completely nonjudgmental, and it made me want to regard all things about her in the same nonjudgmental way.

As she took my hand and led us back up the slippery walkway, I was aware that just as I had guessed on the terrace, Teresa liked me because I was so very different from her husband. In me she had already sensed a kindness and an acceptance that she secretly longed for in her marriage. I was already completing something in her that allowed both of us to ascend the hill to the hotel with a certain degree of anticipation about what might happen as we reached the summit and the familiar veranda where we had cocktails just hours before.

"Do you have any brandy?" she asked when we reached the top.

"No brandy, but I do have some Canadian whiskey."

"That will do. Mostly we need to get out of these wet clothes."

I had no idea what she meant by that, but without any discussion we entered the side door of the hotel and walked down the long corridor to my room. As we entered I was reminded of my paralysis of indecision just ninety minutes earlier, and how I could have scarcely guessed that my return would not be alone, but rather, with Teresa.

"I'm getting a hot shower."

She disappeared into the bathroom, carefully shutting the door until it latched. I sat on the bed and listened as the muffled sound of the shower filled the space in the room.

There may have been a time ten or fifteen years earlier when I would have jumped to all sorts of wild assumptions about what might happen next. But I had learned through countless awkward situations that to assume or expect anything was folly. The best thing to do was literally to do nothing. It relieved the tension and allowed life to occur with all its possibilities fully intact.

She emerged from the bathroom wearing a white terry-cloth robe that had been hanging on the back of the door. Her hair was wrapped in a white terry-cloth towel, and her face was flush from the warmth of the shower.

"Why don't you get a shower and that will give me a few minutes to dry my hair?"

"If you want a drink, the whiskey is on the nightstand," I said, as nonchalantly as possible about having a married woman in my bedroom in the middle of the night. But, as yet, I reasoned, Teresa and I were still just acquaintances who had been thrown together by the unlikeliest of circumstances.

When I turned off the shower I could hear her talking to someone on the phone. Whoever she was talking to was very upset, and she just kept repeating, "You have got to calm down." Of course it was Richard, and I immediately wondered if he had somehow discovered that she was in my room. Either way, I thought of my own stupidity in inserting myself into their marital quarrels. I was in complete violation of my own dictum of not getting involved, and I thought longingly of how I could at this moment be sleeping quietly in the comfort of my bed if I had not ventured out just one hour before. Perhaps vainly hoping for an easy resolution to the conflict, I buttoned up my pajamas and quietly opened the bathroom door.

Teresa was propped up on my bed underneath the mosquito netting with a mountain of pillows behind her and the phone just inches away from her right hand. She was one of those women who look really put together even with damp hair, and I couldn't help but notice one of her long, beautiful legs as it was languidly revealed from the folds of her robe.

"Were you talking on the phone?"

"Richard called. He must have awakened and was worried I hadn't returned. As a last resort he called here to talk to you, and of course I answered the phone."

"So, I assume you are headed back over?"

"Nope. I told Richard I would see him in the morning."

"But you really can't stay here until morning."

"Why not?"

"Look, Teresa. You are a married woman and I don't want to come between you and your husband."

"You aren't coming between us in any way. Richard knows that I have both male and female friends that I love to be with. He's angry now, but he'll be fine in the morning."

My mind raced back to my initial impressions of Teresa on the airplane. She was completely independent and fearless. In my bed was a tigress—a lithe African animal with the magnetism to attract both men and women alike. And now Richard was her cuckold, seemingly helpless to control her. I pitied him as I now began to pity myself for my insertion into this African savanna of survival, where the natural laws of the veld dictate that all animal confrontations end in either disgrace or death.

"Aren't you coming to bed?"

And now I felt like the one who had been cleverly trapped as prey. My heart was pounding. I suddenly felt completely out of my league, and in that fog of confusion I remembered another line from Hemingway that the opposite of fear is beauty.

I slid in next to her and allowed myself to accept her tenderness and warmth, the softness of her embrace. My heart was still pounding, but as our legs intertwined it became an intoxication, a euphoria where I allowed myself to be completely given over to her sheer physicality and her magnificent beauty. Neither of us said a word, but when we both awakened several hours later the sun was streaming in through the glass-paned door that led out to the small deck. What had occurred between us now seemed in complete harmony with all of the events of the previous day—our chance meeting on the airplane, dinner at the hotel, the falls at 1:00 A.M., and holding each other after the bizarre conversation she had with Richard on the phone.

But I was already formulating my exit plan. The yellow lights in my head were blinking wildly at breakfast when Teresa dared to mention to Richard that she had slept better than she had slept in weeks. His eyes had darted across the table—first at Teresa, then at me. I felt ashamed and embarrassed for both of them.

They and their children were scheduled for a boat ride above the falls late that morning, and I somehow begged off from Teresa's persistent invitations to join them. I promised to meet them again for dinner, but as soon as they were gone I packed up and checked out of my room. The next train for Harare was not leaving until 3:00 P.M., so I stored my luggage at the hotel and walked over to the magnificent bridge that Cecil Rhodes had built across the Zambezi in 1906, a key link in the Cape to Cairo railway envisioned at the height of British colonialism. Standing on the bridge and watching the constant parade of bungee jumpers, I could see the walkway that Teresa and I had navigated the night before and the small observation platform where I had found her.

As I walked back to the hotel, the Flight of Angels lumbered overhead, and I suddenly felt an intense loneliness that often arrives unexpectedly when I repeat a pattern of behavior that has left me feeling empty in the past. I saw myself in several hours, sitting on the train and staring out of the window, happy for my breakaway from a potentially messy relationship, but sad because the trajectory of my life had not moved an inch from where it was a month ago or five years before. I was moving through space and time, but my moral compass had only moved from magnetism to magnetism, destined only to point me to the next misadventure that would ultimately bring the same sense of loneliness that had been the motivating influence in the first place.

I reached the hotel lobby; Teresa was standing at the front desk, undoubtedly now aware that I had checked out. By her body language I guessed that she was asking for forwarding information related to my checkout, and the concierge was becoming annoyed at her persistence.

Unfortunately, he also had the keys to the luggage closet. I glanced at my watch. It was 2:47. My train was scheduled to depart in less than fifteen minutes, and the station was a five-minute walk from the hotel. Teresa continued to linger.

Not knowing what I was going to say to her, I finally approached the concierge with about five minutes to go before the train departed.

"James, we have been looking all over for you!" She said it as if I was a recalcitrant child who was lost on the playground.

"I have a gift for you, James. Something I should have given you last night."

The concierge now turned away to help another customer.

"That's sweet of you, Teresa, but I'm actually on the three o'clock train to Bulawayo and then on to Harare. Something's come up."

At that Teresa took her hand and lightly touched my face, repeating the same action that she had made exiting the plane.

"There must be a later train," she said, almost whispering.

And although we were standing in the hotel lobby, I felt completely enveloped by her physicality.

She sensed that I was hesitating.

"You saved me last night, James; I don't want you to leave."

I checked my watch. It was 3:03. I got my bags from the concierge, booked another room, and headed down the corridor to unpack. I wasn't leaving Victoria Falls that evening. It felt as if I might be there forever.

CHAPTER TWO

CHARLIE BENJAMIN GLANCED AT THE CONSOLE CLOCK of his BMW 5 series coupe.

"Almost 1:00 A.M.," he thought.

He had left Winnetka almost five hours earlier, and the blur of St. Paul, Minnesota, signs on I-94 had moved almost imperceptibly from three hundred miles to thirty.

He had originally planned to leave Winnetka at 4:00 or 5:00 P.M. at the latest, but the home health-care worker caring for his father had shown up late, and Ryan's indoor soccer game had gone into overtime.

"Keep your phone on," Heather had shouted from the upstairs balcony, and Charlie had blown her a kiss, a gesture that both of them had found ironic in its perfunctory acknowledgement that they hadn't connected in weeks, and now he was heading to Canada chasing a hunch that he might finally meet his real father after thirty-eight years of blissfully believing that Richard Benjamin was his biological dad.

His partners at Williston, Hughes and Meyers had expressed moderate concern when he told them that he would not be back until the following Monday, and he felt a modicum of guilt that he had concocted a story about going to Alberta to help Heather's brother in his transition to single parenthood. Heather's brother actually lived in British Columbia, but Charlie was confident that once he mentioned Canada, all of the particulars would dissolve into a general accession that he would not return for almost a week.

He thought about his last extended absence from the firm: the ten days in October that he spent in New York with his mother—"the death shroud visit"—in Room 317 at Sloan Kettering, where he had camped out for thirty-six hours, holding his mother's hand as she quietly slipped away.

Even at age seventy, his mother, Teresa, was still a beauty. In the months before she died, she insisted on ordering new clothes from Saks, and two days before she died, she wore an azure blue Hermes silk scarf that Charlie had helped her to carefully tie around the nape of her neck to accent her white cardigan sweater, carefully buttoned as if she had received death's invitation complete with a suggested dress code. The day that she died was one of those late October Indian summer days in New York when the entire city seems to relish New York's prized location at the southwestern tip of New England. A city and a climate with a destiny for all things bright and prosperous—the shadows of the skyscrapers carefully outlining the design of success that seemed especially lucid on a day perfectly balanced between the onslaught of winter and the intoxicating vestige of late summer.

On the third floor of Sloan Kettering, you can hear the ubiquitous honks of taxis and the shrill of police whistles moving along 64th Street—the constant flow of humanity just three floors below. It was somehow appropriate that Teresa Benjamin chose to die on an exquisite autumn afternoon when the bright rays of sunlight were able to mask for one last time the changing of the seasons.

An hour before her death, with Charlie at her side, her eyes suddenly widened as if she were actually glimpsing the prism of eternity that was now filtering into the room.

"Charlie, come close to me."

Her voice was at a whisper, and as her son hovered over her, she seemed to gather herself for a proclamation that she had waited a lifetime to reveal.

"Charlie, Richard loves you dearly, but he is not your real father. Your real father is a man named James Monroe who I slept with in Africa."

The room was completely still save for the street sounds below. It was one of those moments fraught with meaning that struggles to find a context, and in the seconds that passed with her face so very close to his, he managed to respond with his deep love for her that transcended the sterility of the room and even her earlier courage to finally reveal the truth.

"It's OK, Mom."

The two of them sat quietly after that, allowing the import of what had just occurred to distill into their final moments together.

"Does he know about me?"

But Teresa was already gone; content that her son finally knew the truth, she was now ready to accept the end of her fantastic life. Charlie sat there alone with her for twenty minutes until a nurse finally arrived to check on her patient.

"Does he know about me?"

His mother had gone to her grave without answering the question.

Charlie was racing across central Minnesota, the lights of St. Paul now way off to the southeast. The recollection of his mother's death—and even more, the profundity of her life—had managed to envelop him once again, and he realized North Dakota was ahead and by mid-morning he would be in eastern Montana. It was a clear night and the March sky was a crescent of starlight. Already the horizon had lengthened out and Charlie noticed fewer and fewer cars. He clicked on the radio and found an AM station from Montreal. It was signing off for the night, and the crackled sound of the La Marseillaise, the French National Anthem, played faintly in the darkness.

Charlie thought of his own French-Canadian heritage. Teresa had been raised in Montreal, and her mother, who had the French name "Therese," migrated from Paris to Canada after the Second World War. Teresa's father died in France—a war victim of embedded shrapnel that eventually led to heart failure. His death awakened an entrepreneurial self-sufficiency in Therese, and she soon became the proprietor of several successful boutiques in Old Montreal. When Teresa completed her secondary education in Canada, she was bilingual, and her penchant for art and art history drew her to Manhattan, where she matriculated at Columbia, a young French-Canadian sophisticate who soon found her way into art openings and receptions where New York's corporate scions intersected with aspiring artists from Manhattan and beyond.

It was at one of these openings on the Upper West Side that Teresa met Richard. He had recently earned his MBA from the University of Pennsylvania, and he represented a financial worldview that Teresa found both fascinating and (later) incredibly boring. Once they began dating, what Richard lacked in artistic imagination he made up for in his chatter about market buybacks and potential cash flow. He had the knowledge base to hold his own among the elite of Wall Street, and Teresa reasoned that if he knew this much about other people's money, he would undoubtedly be equally facile with his own.

It wasn't until year three of their marriage that Teresa discovered that Richard's theoretical expertise was not matched by an equally potent business acumen. Shortly after their wedding, Teresa's mother had given him a considerable sum to invest in American markets, and eighteen months later, he had lost thirty percent of its original value. Richard blamed market volatility, but Teresa sensed a pattern. Her husband talked a good game, but he lacked both the scrutiny and the timing to be a successful broker.

They compensated by acquiring the trappings of wealth, but it was a veneer that was paper thin. They borrowed money to go on expensive trips—to Europe, to Africa—and Richard refused frugality even when his income dictated a more modest lifestyle. Teresa suspected that she was a better money manager than her husband, and when income was low, it was often her resourcefulness that rescued them. Instead of being grateful, these moments of financial crisis caused Richard to become insular and bitter. He saw her intercessions as a usurpation of his authority, and his disdain often manifested itself in fits of anger that further compromised their marriage.

Charlie's two older brothers had gone to prep school, but by the time he was fifteen, whatever money had been set aside for his tuition was long gone. He attributed his own lack of confidence to a high school experience where he was anonymous in a graduating class of four hundred. Richard made up some story about why Charlie preferred to stay home from boarding school, and Charlie always felt complicit in Richard's elaborate cover-up.

By the time Charlie was almost out of high school, Teresa had resigned herself—as many women do—to a static marital relationship. There was an undercurrent of disappointment and regret that relegated her more to the role of caretaker than spouse. Charlie gradually became the full object of her affection, and the youthful exuberance that characterized the early years of her marriage was now resurrected and redirected to her son. Charlie essentially replaced Richard as the primary man in Teresa's life, and reawakened in Richard the latent suspicion that he was not Charlie's biological father.

Charlie's job at Williston, Hughes and Meyers was one that Teresa had landed for him through her friendship with Meg Williston. Everyone at the firm suspected that Charlie had been hired because of an inside connection, and they were pleasantly surprised when he turned out to be adept at bringing in new clients. But his job was not fireproof. The culture of the firm punished lack of productivity by withholding year-end bonuses or by not inviting laggards to key client events. "Slugs" were drummed out on a regular basis. When Charlie was hired, Heather became a valuable asset to the firm. Her breezy demeanor and good looks were perfect for drawing in new business. She had a measured flirtatiousness that suggested to prospects that they were the reason for her vivacity.

Lately, however, Heather had become more subdued, often attending events at the firm in an obligatory manner. Customers became aware of her scarcely feigned interest, and privately Charlie lied to colleagues that Heather's ennui was due to exhaustion or concern for her recently divorced brother. But Heather's indifference began to seep its way into even the most banal details of their marriage, and Charlie found himself in a defensive posture most of the time. This evolved into a passive-aggressive demeanor, which allowed him a secret satisfaction that he was not being subsumed by Heather's slide into emotional mediocrity. He often forced himself to be cheerfully upbeat in direct contrast to her sullen moodiness.

His motivation for driving west was partly fueled by his curiosity regarding his real father, but it was also a reprieve from a deteriorating marriage. Neither of them knew how to stop the bleeding. He thought of Heather and Ryan fast asleep back in Winnetka, and how they would soon be waking up for another day of school and soccer. They were his identity, but as he headed west on I-94, something else was drawing him. He couldn't help but feel that he was finally headed home.

CHAPTER THREE

I ORDERED ROOM SERVICE FOR MY DINNER THAT EVENING AS well as breakfast the next morning. The last thing I wanted was to have another encounter with Teresa and her family, so I was chagrined to find that the next train to Bulawayo and Harare would not leave until late in the day on Saturday. That presented another full day and a half at The Victoria Falls Hotel, and after telephoning Nairobi to check in with AFREA, I wandered across the bridge, which is just below the falls, and entered Zambia on the other side. The Zambia side has more of a park-like feel to it, the result, I surmised, of that country's intention to protect the natural surroundings of the falls. I followed a small path to a sign which read "The Devil's Pool," and about fifty yards down the path was a clearing where I saw three or four people standing frightfully close to the edge of the falls and three or four others literally swimming in a small whirlpool that was producing a counteractive flow to the water rushing over the edge. The sound of the water at the lip of the falls was deafening, and it added to the drama of the Devil's Pool.

The sight of it somehow reminded me of Teresa in all of her fearlessness and her willingness, in the right circumstances, to cheat death. Two of the women in the pool were laughing and talking as if they were pond swimming on a July afternoon, while the lone man kept peering over the edge as if to reassure himself that the counteractive flow of the pool would continue to keep him in check.

The people standing on the edge of the bank were clearly waiting for the first group to emerge from the pool so that they could have their turn. I must have appeared completely mesmerized, and I didn't respond immediately when one of them turned to me.

"Ready to have a go?"

"I don't have a swimsuit."

He was one of those Brits who move into that four-inch space that normally defines casual conversation, and now his rather large nose seemed somewhat invasive.

"Last time we were here, most of us wore our boxers." He said it in such a way as to imply that he was already a member of the Devil's Pool society, and my initiation would be to wear my boxers as if to prove my own virility and lack of fear.

One of the women who was standing a few feet away now also turned in my direction.

"Are you going to have a go?"

I realized that this was the initiation question that they were all going to revert to as they introduced themselves. It was the question of the morning, and as I moved closer to the three of them, I surmised that my brief conversation had been with two British expats who were undoubtedly husband and wife. The young woman standing next to them peered across the lip of the falls to the pool, and from where I was standing, it was impossible to see whether her stare was one of curiosity or fear.

Glimpses of sunlight were now punctuated by occasional shafts of small rainbows as the thunderous spray from below created a constant mist to form at the top of the falls. Part of the attraction of the Devil's Pool was the changing patterns of mist and sunlight that seemed to shift one's perception of distance. Already the pool seemed almost twice as far away as when I first arrived.

Looking up the riverbank I could see crocodiles sunning themselves one hundred meters in the distance, just out of range of the swell of current that would sweep them over if they ventured too far from the bank. It occurred to me that their reptilian instincts for nature's boundaries were not shared by those already in the pool and by the foursome, which now included me, as we waited our turn on the bank. I had tarried too long to now make a graceful exit, and I thought of how a similar moment of indecision had caused me to miss my train.

"Hi, I'm Melissa."

"James, James Monroe."

"What brings you to Victoria Falls? Surely not the Devil's Pool?"

Her accent was different from the British couple, and as she spoke the soft curve of her upper lip seemed to release the words one by one as if she were presenting them to the world for the first time.

"You're not from the UK."

"And neither are you," she countered.

"I'm guessing Australia, though many Americans would not know the difference."

"Melbourne, actually," and again her words hung in the air, their import increasing second by second. "I'm here with my sister and her husband on holiday. And you?"

"I work for the World Bank—currently working out of Nairobi, but I've had interviews this past week in Harare."

"And today you're interviewing someone at the Devil's Pool?"

There was a playfulness, even a lightheartedness about her that was immediately attractive.

"I'm actually here to interview you."

"And I'm assuming all of your interviews take place in the pool and not at the water's edge?"

At that she pulled off her white lace cotton top and stepped out of her sandals. She was wearing a black nylon one-piece stretch suit that revealed her long legs and the lovely curve of her back. Her long brown hair was slightly curled, and it fell across her shoulders in such a way that suggested a certain carelessness and confidence that Australian women are known for.

She was already up to her knees when her brother-in-law shouted at her to return to the bank.

"The pool can't hold all of us. Let the others come back first."

But Melissa was undeterred. As the three of us watched she made her way out into the current before turning to flash me a quick smile. The safe strategy to enter the pool was from the more shallow side nearer to the bank, but Melissa was already swimming across the current to approach the pool either straight on or slightly to the side where the water cascaded unchecked over the falls.

As she guided herself into the current that appeared to head directly for the pool, the man who had been sitting on the farthest edge began to wave his arm to get Melissa's attention. He was attempting at the same time to move closer to the far edge, but because of the force of the whirlpool, his movements appeared clumsy and in slow motion.

As Melissa began to pick up speed it was obvious that the current was pulling her off to the right and away from the pool itself. Sensing that her current trajectory would take her over the falls, she began to swim furiously back against the current, but despite her athleticism she was only just holding her own or even losing her struggle with the swells of the current.

The man in the pool was now making slow progress in moving in her direction, and he began to shout at her, but whatever he said was inaudible in the deafening roar. The three of us on the bank could have attempted to swim in after her, but instead we were paralyzed by the quick succession of events that now had Melissa swimming for her life.

The man in the pool was pointing to a large rock that was outside the pool and perilously close to the lip of the falls. As Melissa continued to swim against the current, we could see her body tiring, her strokes becoming less emphatic. Whether she heard the man's shouts or not was impossible to tell, but she was now somewhat adrift and heading for the lip of the falls. The distance from the edge of the pool to the rock at the top of the falls was about ten feet, and we watched in amazement as the man in the pool swam out of the top of the pool and into the current. Summoning all of his strength, he guided his body in the direction of the rock, and despite crashing into the rock with considerable force, he managed to find a handhold and stabilize himself for the attempt to rescue Melissa.

Melissa now disappeared beneath the ripples of the current, and it was clear that the man had lost sight of her. He was frantically looking to his left and right, and now he seemed to be losing his grip on the rock. Her head now broke the surface of the water. She was only ten feet from the rock, but the current was pulling her off to the right. The man somehow shifted his weight to the right, and sensing that he would have only one opportunity to save her, he planted himself face first and extended his right arm as far as he could into the current.

As her form came into his peripheral vision, he made a final lunge into the current, just grasping her left wrist as she hurtled by—now only a few feet from the lip of the falls. The touch of his hand on her wrist must have shot a final burst of adrenaline into Melissa, and as her head resurfaced, she somehow managed to bring her right arm over the top of her body and grasp his arm just below the elbow.

The two of them hung there for several seconds until the man slowly began to flex his right elbow—an act of incredible strength—the result being that Melissa was drawn that much closer to him, and now her head was fully out of the current. He locked his elbow in this akimbo position, and we could see the taut muscles of his back straining to hold on. Melissa slid her left forearm over this human lever and now they were locked elbow to elbow—a position that offered her the leverage she needed to shift her body closer to the rock. She somehow managed to bend her knees and draw her legs into a tight ball, which reduced the force of the current rushing by her. Her feet were now touching the side of the rock and her head was pressed into the man's side.

Using the strength of her legs to her advantage, she lunged across the top of his shoulders and found the crevices in the rock just next to his head. As if the two of them had practiced this rescue attempt before, he began to move inch by inch to his left as she did the same, gingerly finding the small handholds in the rock. She now shifted her body so that she was stretched fully across his back, and they both allowed the current to plant them securely together so that she was now fully on top of him, her black nylon suit pressed into the blades of his back. She shifted a little, and now their heads were next to each other as they both faced the rock and the lip of the falls. This proved to be a distinct advantage, as they were now able to speak to one another in calmer tones and to plan a strategy that would complete the rescue. They stayed in that position for several minutes, obviously intent on regaining their strength before continuing on.

"Shouldn't we call for some help?"

I realized how feeble my contribution seemed after watching Melissa emerge from certain death.

"No one to call on the Zambia side. They have patrols but most of the time they can't be reached."

My British friend seemed completely resigned that the final steps of the rescue would be only up to Melissa and her rescuer. He sounded as if we were watching the final minutes of a soccer match where the goalkeeper would be relied upon to get his team through the last critical surge from the opposing team. Watching them locked in their odd embrace, I was made aware of the strange mixture of courage, athleticism, and sensuality that we had been privy to as observers on the riverbank.

The rescue for Melissa and the man had become a private, desperate struggle for life itself. Their ability to work in perfect tandem had allowed them to slip through the smallest opportunity for safety. Only ten minutes earlier they had been complete strangers. Now their bodies pressed together and their faces touched as they whispered what to do next.

As if in celebration, the sun again broke through the clouds, sending sparkles of refracted light across the gap between the rock and the Devil's Pool. Sensing the blinding sunlight as a sign, the two of them began to inch their way to the point on the rock that was closest to the pool. Their plan became clear. She would go first, pushing off from the rock and swimming upstream, and he would follow after her, putting himself between her and the danger of sliding over the falls.

As it had been earlier, their plan was perfectly executed. The arc of her trajectory allowed him to intercept her exhausted body just a meter away from the pool. The two women were waiting for them as close to the pool's edge as they dared, and at the last possible moment he lunged—with Melissa on his back—out of the current and into the pool.

"Well done," my British friend shouted as if he had been some ancillary part of the strategy of the rescue.

The two women held Melissa between them, one of them holding Melissa's head on her shoulder as a mother would hold a child. The streams of sunlight breaking through the mist at the top of the pool surrounded the three of them as if in a religious tableau. As Melissa lifted her head from the woman's shoulder, she briefly appeared to be floating above the pool, the mist surrounding her feet. Her face was glowing from the exhilaration of the rescue, and there was a calmness about her that was also eerily religious.

I have only directly encountered the supernatural a few times in my life, but all of us on the bank were witnessing a kind of apotheosis—Melissa's triumphant re-entry into life after her dramatic encounter with death. Her moment of transcendence was accentuated by the light, the roar of the falls, and the evanescent mist which constantly shifted our perspective. Her rescuer was half submerged in the pool and his gaze was also fixed on Melissa's face, as if he was paying homage to the woman who had reconfirmed his innate prowess, his ability to alter a certain course of events simply by his will and his incredible strength.

I didn't want to be there standing with the others when Melissa returned to the safety of the riverbank. The events of her rescue instead left me feeling incredibly inadequate, and as I walked back up the path I knew that I was secretly jealous of the adrenaline rush that they had experienced together. I kept seeing their bodies pressed together against the rock, the two of them, total strangers, sharing their primal desire for survival, a union of selfless physicality that redefined their humanity to a place just below the gods.

That evening I ventured out of my room around five o'clock and headed to the bar, which was just off the lobby. I knew that Teresa and Richard wouldn't venture down for cocktails until at least six, and I was looking forward to being out of my room and anonymous for at least an hour. To my surprise, Melissa was sitting alone at a table next to the window, a book in her left hand as the fingers of her right hand lightly touched the stem of her cocktail glass.

"I wasn't expecting to see you here."

Melissa barely looked up. "I was just reading about what to do if you find yourself being carried over the falls."

"I didn't know that Camus had been to Victoria Falls."

Melissa smiled and slowly creased the book over her left wrist so that L'Etranger came clearly into view.

"Haven't you had enough existentialism for one day?"

"It's the human condition that fascinates me—you know, all of us estranged from one another and estranged from ourselves." It was the first philosophical insight I'd heard in weeks. "Why don't you sit down, James."

I was beginning to think that Melissa actually was a goddess—someone who could master any physical challenge and philosophically encapsulate the human condition in one sentence.

"Do you believe that is true?"

"Of course it's true."

"That we live in a state of estrangement?"

"We all make do. We all construct a habitation that makes it bearable."

Without even turning around I sensed that Teresa was in the room, and I realized that my sharing a table with Melissa was about to complicate matters even further.

"Good evening, James." It was an icy salutation and one in complete contrast to her greeting on the terrace two nights before.

"We looked for you all day today. We started to fear that you had gone swimming in the Zambezi and had been sucked over the falls."

"Teresa, I'd like to you to meet a friend of mine from Australia, Melissa Samuel."

I hoped that the ambiguity of my introduction would be enough, but Teresa pressed on.

"So the two of you are old friends?"

"Actually we just met today. We were both satisfying our curiosity about the Devil's Pool—over on the Zambia side."

"We may have seen you. We took a launch on the Zambia side and had a tour of the crocodiles sunning themselves at the river's edge."

"Sounds dangerous, to say the least."

But before Teresa could reply, one of her children, her eldest son, appeared at her side.

"I think I'm being summoned to the terrace. Nice to meet you, Miss Samuel. Perhaps we'll see you and James later this evening?"

Teresa lightly touched my shoulder before following her son through the French doors that led to the hotel terrace. In doing so, she was telegraphing to Melissa our pre-existing relationship and she was indirectly reminding me of our intimacy of two nights before.

Either Melissa didn't notice Teresa's parting gesture, or it had little effect.

"I feel like taking a walk. Nothing too strenuous. I've probably had enough exercise for one day."

As we made our way down the path to the falls, I once again noticed Melissa's athleticism. Even her walk had a certain grace to it that made her every movement appear effortless. As we approached the same platform where Teresa had been standing when I found her crying, I noticed that the evening sun was casting long shadows into the gorge. The top of the falls was completely illuminated, and there was a rainbow just above the lip where the dying sunlight and the spray intermingled in an ever-changing panorama of water and light.

It was one of those moments of perfect balance when our internal sense of harmony and freedom is realized and inspired by our external reality—even if that reality is temporary and fleeting. The nexus of that moment was the evening sun on the falls, but it was also Melissa, and I thought of her after the rescue also illuminated by sunlight, floating goddess-like over the Devil's Pool.

"Who else do you read other than Camus?"

The beauty of the moment had led me back to her earlier statement about the estrangement of existence.

"I read the three Ds—Dante, Dostoevsky, and Disraeli."

"I get Dante and Dostoevsky, but why Benjamin Disraeli?"

"Because to date he has been the only Jewish Prime Minister of England, and he was both a civil servant and a novelist."

"What did he write?"

"His best-known novel is *Endymion*."

Once again I noticed, as I had earlier, that Melissa was able to speak certain words and phrases with a clarity that made them more emphatic and compelling. I hadn't read *Endymion*, but the way she pronounced the title made it seem as if Disraeli had written a novel for the ages.

"Endymion from Greek mythology was the same Endymion from the Keats poem—the shepherd king who was so remarkably beautiful that the moon, Selene, fell in love with him. She asked Zeus to make Endymion forever young, so Zeus granted him eternal sleep and gave Selene permission to visit him every night. Endymion is both deathless and ageless. Disraeli's novel is more social and political, whereas Keats' fascination was with Endymion's beauty and his eternal state of sleep. We share that with him, of course—sleeping into eternity."

As we climbed back up the path together I realized that Melissa had a moral imagination that she was able to call upon in any circumstance. There was an intuitive wisdom about her that was completely disarming, and the effect on me was nothing less than spellbinding. Reaching the shadows of the hotel, I did not want the night to end. Realizing that Teresa and Richard would likely be in the lobby or in the bar, I boldly suggested to Melissa that we decamp to my room.

"Lead the way, James."

The tone of her voice was one of quiet confidence—even serenity. Could it be possible that her intuitive understanding of the human condition included the ability to quickly perceive individual character and motivation? Shortly after arriving in my room, Melissa climbed onto my bed fully clothed and fell asleep. I carefully draped the mosquito netting around the perimeter, then poured a whiskey and simply watched her as she slept. This was the nightly vigil that Selene had with Endymion—only now we had switched genders and I was the one sitting in quiet adoration of Melissa. The mythological parallel was striking, and for the first time in years I felt a part of something greater than myself. It was her mystery that held me in captivity, and like Selene I was drawn to that dreamlike reverie where beauty is both ageless and timeless. I have known the disappointing fragility of love and how it can evaporate without warning. So this state of eternal contemplation without consummation is the one place where love can thrive with a fervor that is never abated, with a passion that is forever vibrant and transcendent.

CHAPTER FOUR

"ANYONE HOME?"

The sound of his own voice in the stillness of the Canadian dawn seemed alone and distant.

"Anyone here?"

Charlie knocked slightly at the large oak door and to his surprise it opened a crack just enough for him to see a sliver of light, possibly coming from the back of the house.

He paused, still clutching the small piece of paper that had James Monroe's address in Lake Louise, and now his marathon drive from Chicago began to seem even more ridiculous if he had driven thirty hours only to arrive at an empty house. A woman's voice (he would never have heard her if the door had been completely shut) could now be heard from the second floor.

"Be down in a minute."

After several minutes he began to think he had only imagined that someone was actually there.

"I'm Jenny Monroe."

"Charlie Benjamin."

He had been expecting to see his real father for the first time, but instead he was greeted by a strikingly beautiful woman who must have been in her late forties or early fifties, wearing an exotic Asian silk robe decorated with colorful scenes of a Chinese princess. All this Charlie noticed in the split second between their greeting and his quickly formulated explanation of why he was there.

"Is this the home of James Monroe?"

"James Monroe is my father; I'm his daughter, Jenny. Papa isn't home right now, but I would be happy to let him know that you stopped by to see him."

Charlie now realized that he was speaking to his half sister, but he quickly revised his explanation of why he was there.

"My mother and your father were once very close friends. My mother died recently, and one of her last requests was that I would visit your father to tell him in person how much she cared for him. It is so presumptive of me to show up here unannounced. My mother gave me this address before she died—actually, I found it in her purse the morning of her death. I thought that the very least I could do was to honor one of her last wishes."

"How very sweet."

As she invited Charlie into the small downstairs hallway, she was racking her brain, searching for how her father (who never remarried after his divorce) might have known this man's mother in such a profound way.

"What was your mother's name?"

"Teresa Benjamin. She passed away just six months ago. I think they met in Africa, but that's all I really know."

The smell of coffee and freshly baked rolls filled the hallway and the adjoining parlor, and the warmth of the fireplace reminded Charlie of summers that he had spent in northern Michigan at a lake camp owned by his grandparents.

Leaving him standing in the parlor (she had already offered him a chair) Jenny returned to the kitchen. Charlie couldn't tell if the tone in her voice was one of incredulity or simple curiosity. While she went back to the kitchen to bring them coffee, he surveyed the room and noticed pictures of his father with a much younger Jenny. One of the photographs was of the two of them standing in front of the opening of a cave. His father had both of his hands on her shoulders and she was looking at him with a gaze of adoration.

On the opposite wall were several photos from what appeared to be Africa. There was his father standing with a small group of people on a riverbank with mist and spray in the background. His father was standing next to a woman—at first he thought it was his mother—but the woman was taller than Teresa and more athletic looking.

Jenny appeared with a tray of coffee and fresh rolls and Charlie finally sat down, keenly aware of the awkwardness of having breakfast with his half sister while she regarded him as a complete stranger.

"You're being very kind to someone you just met a few minutes ago."

"It's odd; the moment you walked in I had a quick flash that we had met before."

As Jenny sat across from him, Charlie was again taken with her beauty. In her haste to get dressed she had pulled back her long black hair and secured it with a porcelain clip that matched the Chinese pattern in her robe. She even looked oriental with her high cheekbones and dark green eyes, and there was an openness and a sincerity about her that helped him to feel more at ease. He remembered his intuition as he raced across Minnesota that his arrival would be well received.

"I'm sorry to hear about your mother."

They both paused for a moment, almost as a tribute to Teresa's life.

It was the first of three or four opportunities during Charlie's two-day stay when he was tempted to tell Jenny the truth. They both had the same father. They were both children of divorce. And despite Charlie being married, he had the same angst of unfinished business that he was beginning to sense in Jenny.

"Jenny, tell me about your mother."

The question hung in the air for a moment and Charlie hoped he had not been too intrusive.

"After my parents' divorce, I only saw my mother three or four times a year—mostly on major holidays. It was always awkward since my mother eventually married my father's best friend. He didn't have his own children, so there was this charade that we were somehow a little family. He always kissed me on my forehead at the end of my visits as if to suggest there was some latent affection there, but I resented him. He tried to act in a way that he imagined my father might act, but he was nothing like my father. I lived with my father from age ten until I left for college, and I am as close to him as a father and daughter could possibly be. Mother died six years ago. Papa went to the funeral, but I couldn't bring myself to attend. I knew my stepfather would be offering platitudes that would be phony and insincere."

Charlie's cell phone went off and he realized it was probably Heather wanting to know if he had safely arrived. For reasons that he couldn't immediately identify, he didn't want to talk to Heather with Jenny sitting right there. Jenny already represented a new world that he was related to by paternity. He was the only one living who knew the secret, but he already knew that he would find a way to tell Jenny the truth while he was in Lake Louise. He didn't know how he would ever fully share the same truth with Heather. It might be met with disdain—or even worse—indifference. He had this odd idea that sharing his real identity with Jenny would create a bond that would be forever mysterious and slightly forbidden. Teresa had carried the secret of his real father for almost forty years. He wanted to respect the integrity of a reality that she had carefully guarded for a lifetime.

"You must be exhausted. Thirty hours of driving must have taken its toll. Why don't you take a nap in Papa's room? He often gives up his bed for unexpected visitors, and I'm sure he won't mind. I'll wake you up for dinner."

One disadvantage of living in the high peaks of the Canadian Rockies is the light that is lost in the late afternoon as the mountains block out the sun. Lake Louise is no exception, and even in early March it begins to get dark by four o'clock. Charlie climbed the small flight of wooden stairs and entered his father's bedroom. Over the bed was a wooden cross and in the corner were snowshoes and cross-country skis. The entire room had an austerity about it that suggested asceticism. There was a lamp and a writing desk and over the desk hung a brightly colored sash that looked like it belonged to a sari. Remembering Heather's call, he sent a text to her that immediately bounced back with a "No Service" message. Normally he would have explored the house searching for a signal, but instead he collapsed on the bed, not even removing his shoes, and fell fast asleep.

Charlie awakened in complete darkness to the smell of pot roast and potatoes. At first he thought he was in his own bedroom at home. He glanced at his phone. Three missed calls. He had to call Heather before she called the Canadian Mounted Police. Charlie wandered downstairs holding his phone, hoping to find at least one bar. He slipped on his coat and walked toward his car. Two bars. He navigated to call history and selected his home phone.

"Thank God, you're alive." It was the way Heather answered calls from Charlie when he neglected to call her from work.

"I'm in Lake Louise. I got here this morning, but I've had phone issues." Charlie suddenly remembered that it was six at home because of the time difference. "Did Ryan have indoor soccer?"

"Of course he had indoor soccer; it's Thursday."

From the sound of her voice he could tell that she was already resenting his absence, especially because of the additional parent duties when he was away.

"But how are you doing? Is everything OK?"

Charlie braced himself for her response, knowing that she would reel off a litany of all the ways that she had been inconvenienced since he left. He patiently listened.

"Sounds like you've had your hands full." Heather paused to make her reply even more emphatic.

"Is that all you've got to say? How about 'I know you must be struggling and I'll make it up to you when I get home'?"

Heather had cornered him like this so many times recently that he knew that any response would be met with criticism.

"Look, I know that parenting is difficult when I'm not there, and I will make it up to you."

They were both silent for almost a minute. Charlie just wanted to end it and get off the phone. He could see Jenny through the window, still wearing her Chinese robe and arranging wine glasses and hors d'oeuvres on the small table where they had talked that morning.

"Did you find your father?" Heather said it in such a perfunctory way that she might have been talking about Charlie finding a pair of lost glasses.

"Amazingly, I did." He was formulating a lie, knowing that Heather would be incensed if he were staying a few days in the wilds of Canada with a single woman and not his father. "Even though I'm exhausted, we spent most of the day in front of the fire trying to piece back together all that has happened since he and my mother met in Africa."

"When are you coming home?"

"I think we may do some cross-country skiing or snowshoeing tomorrow. I'll probably head for home at some point tomorrow."

"If you could be home by Sunday at noon that would solve so

many problems for me. Otherwise, I'll have to find a babysitter to take Ryan to soccer."

Their calls recently had ended this way, with Heather extracting some extra commitment from Charlie to help her feel she was in control.

"Sounds good," Charlie muttered. "Can't wait to see you and Ryan."

"Call me around this time tomorrow."

As Charlie hung up he noticed that he had five voicemails, all from his office. He thought about listening to them but then noticed the magnificent Alberta sky. The stars were piercing the darkness above the mountains with a radiance that was breathtaking. It was cold—probably only fifteen degrees—and the sight of Jenny preparing dinner and the smoke pouring from the chimney awakened a myriad of emotions. He wanted to tell her this evening that she was not an only child, that they had the same father, that he had never had a sister—especially one who seemed so similar in temperament to himself.

"How was your nap?" Before Charlie could respond, Jenny continued. "Papa loves to take naps in the late afternoons—especially when he has returned from a long week in Vancouver."

Charlie noticed that Jenny had added mauve silk pants to complement her Chinese robe, and despite the stone floor, her feet were bare. There was a casual elegance about her that seemed to reflect the decor of the room.

"What does your father do in Vancouver?"

"He and his friend, Rob, run a halfway house for homeless people. It's exhausting because it's basically just the two of them. It's the turnover that's so work intensive. They limit their guests to one-week stays."

"What happens after a week?"

"There are longer-term facilities in Vancouver. Papa and Rob's place is for people in crisis, but they do help people transition to other facilities. I was there last summer for almost six weeks;

I helped with cooking and housekeeping. The stuff you see is eye-opening."

Charlie thought of the homeless shelter that he passed two or three times a week on his way to Ryan's soccer practice. In the summer there were always middle-aged men sitting out front smoking. Their eyes were vacant, their hair long and greasy. Charlie wondered what life events had brought them to that point. But now, sitting there with Jenny, he wanted to think about something else. As if aware of Charlie's silent request, Jenny headed back towards the kitchen. The smell of pot roast and other spices filled the downstairs, becoming an aperitif to the senses.

"How about a glass of red? I have a lovely Cab from British Columbia."

He watched her as she carefully uncorked the bottle in the kitchen. She took down two oversized wine glasses that sparkled in her hand. As she handed a glass to Charlie, he noticed how her hands were shaped by usefulness, her nails filed fairly close and without polish.

"Cheers."

"To new friends."

As they both took a first sip, Charlie knew that this evening would be the time to tell her their true relationship, but throughout dinner they discussed Charlie's work, Ryan's growing interest in soccer, and the local politics of Lake Louise. It wasn't until Jenny poured him a cognac in lieu of dessert that Charlie mustered up the courage to finally broach the topic.

"Jenny, there must be something I could do for you. You are showing incredible kindness to a stranger who just showed up at your door."

"Papa and I are used to providing for strangers. In fact, that is what he is doing as we speak. Besides, we aren't strangers; Papa and your mother must have been great friends."

It was the perfect segue. Charlie looked at his nearly empty cognac and searched for his next sentence. But before he could speak, Jenny began to get up from the table.

"Actually I do have a small request. I'm going upstairs to take a quick bath. If it isn't too much to ask, I could use some help with the dishes."

She didn't wait for his response, and taking her cognac, she headed up the stairs. Charlie drained his glass and sat for a moment. There was an openness about Jenny that was reminiscent of the way Heather had been in the early years of their marriage. Like Teresa, Heather had always assumed the best about people, and it was her disarming breezy demeanor that allowed her to navigate life by accepting all its vagaries without judgment. Being with her in those nonjudgmental years had provided him a sense of freedom, and he longed for its return. He was willing to accept the changes in Heather that had probably been the result of postpartum depression. What he wasn't able to accept were the changes that Heather's transformation had now imposed on his own worldview. He was becoming a person who he did not want to be: shortsighted, secretive, and plagued by judgment of others as well as himself. In Jenny he immediately sensed a return to freedom, a stay from judgment, and as he cleared the table and began to wash the dishes, a sense of joy welled up within him. For a moment he allowed himself to believe that he lived in western Canada, that his existence in Winnetka was only a dream, and that he was finally closing in on his true identity.

"Can you look on the kitchen counter? I need my phone in case Papa calls."

Jenny was calling him through the open bathroom door. Charlie found her phone, and as he headed up the stairs the smell of lavender and bath oil permeated the small hallway. Jenny was in the clawfoot tub, and as he opened the door a little more he could see the pinpricks of stars in the skylight and the traces of steam on the mirror. He felt like he was entering a sanctuary. Jenny, still immersed in the water, turned slightly and extended her left arm to get the phone. Her long dark hair was still pulled up and clasped with the porcelain clip. As she took the phone with one hand, she unclasped the clip with the other and her hair cascaded around her shoulders.

"Can you hand me the shampoo? I think it may have slid under the tub."

Averting his eyes, Charlie got down on his hands and knees and began feeling under the tub for the shampoo. After several tries, he extended his arm as far as it would go and grasped the elusive bottle.

"My father washed my hair when I was young. It's one of the things I remember from my childhood."

Charlie was amazed that Jenny was completely comfortable with him being so near to her in such an intimate setting, and for a moment he considered asking her if she wanted him to wash her hair. Instead, using the side of the tub as leverage, he pulled himself up and took a step towards the door. It suddenly occurred to him that Jenny might simply exit the bathroom and go right to bed.

"I'll be downstairs. Maybe we could have another cognac in front of the fire."

As Charlie descended the stairs, he thought of Heather's reaction if she knew he had been so close to Jenny in the bathroom and thinking about washing her hair.

"But," he reasoned, "she is my sister, which is different than just some other woman."

When Jenny reappeared a few minutes later, she had on her Chinese robe and her hair was wrapped in a towel. Charlie poured both of them the last of the cognac, and Jenny sat down across from him, enjoying the warmth of the fire on her bare legs and feet.

"Jenny, I need to tell you something."

She had already removed the towel from her head and was attempting to dry sections of her hair by vigorously rubbing them in both directions.

"Oh, by the way," Jenny interrupted, "Thanks for doing the dishes. I end up doing the dishes every evening whether Papa is here or not. So nice to have a break!"

"Jenny, we both have the same father."

She allowed her wet hair to fall in a tangle around her face.

"What?"

"My mother and your father slept together in Africa. That's why I'm here. I came to meet my biological father."

The phrase "biological father" seemed to catch Jenny off guard. Her father was her rock. He was even her soulmate. She was stunned Charlie had referred to him as "biological"—as if her father had been reduced to a chance romantic encounter in Africa.

"That's impossible. I am my father's only child. He doesn't have a son."

"I am your father's son. My mother told me on her deathbed. Her exact words were 'Your real father is a man named James Monroe who I slept with in Africa.'"

"There must be a hundred men named James Monroe who have been to Africa."

"True. And that is why I need to talk to him to be sure."

"To be sure about what?"

"That he remembers sleeping with my mother."

"And if he doesn't?"

"Then I will continue to look."

At that, Jenny pushed away her cognac, as if to say that she was done with the conversation, that she was done with the evening.

"I'm sorry, Jenny. I knew that this would be hard for you to take in after all these years."

"You think we are brother and sister?"

"I think we both have the same father, but of course, different mothers."

"Why did you come here?" Suddenly she was agitated and losing patience.

"A man wants to meet his real father."

"It's presumptuous of you to just show up here. It was crazy of me to allow you to stay here."

"If I could meet your father, we could resolve all of this in a few minutes."

Jenny walked across the room and sat down at the table. Just one hour before Charlie had been seated across from her having dinner. Now he felt like an outsider and an intruder.

"The earliest Papa will be home is Saturday."

"Is there a number where we can call him?"

"It's not the sort of thing you can settle over the phone or by email. You can stay here this evening, but you need to leave first thing in the morning. I can't help you find your father, and I suggest that you don't try to contact Papa. It will just upset him."

At that, Jenny locked the front door and turned out the lights.

"Goodnight, Mr. Benjamin. I suppose we'll see each other in the morning before you leave."

As Jenny headed up the stairs, Charlie sat gazing into the fire. "Maybe she's right," he thought. Maybe this whole idea of finding his real father was a misguided quest that he thought up to address his own sense of ennui. "I may have only done this to get away from Heather for a few days—to break the routine, to find a reprieve."

Charlie fell asleep in the chair, awakened about forty-five minutes later, and headed up to bed. It was one of those evenings when sleep would be his only escape—a brief interlude from a plan that had taken a sudden turn for the worse.

CHAPTER FIVE

I AWAKENED AROUND 3:00 A.M. TO THE SOUND OF RAIN ON the roof. I had fallen asleep in the large ottoman chair, and the only light was from a small lamp in the bathroom. Melissa stirred a little as I turned out the light and returned to the ottoman. The room was now pitch black. The sound of the rain and the distant falls seemed more soothing than I had remembered since my arrival.

About an hour later I awakened again to the sound of Melissa whispering in her sleep. At first, whatever she was saying was garbled and incomprehensible, but as she continued, she began to speak in a language I had never heard before. It sounded like Arabic or ancient Hebrew. At intervals she sat straight up and lengthened her arms out to her sides, allowing her hands to rotate so that her palms seemed to be in adoration or in obeisance to a person or an object.

Engulfed in darkness and separated by the mosquito netting, I listened as she participated in an ancient ritual, her soft voice fluctuating between speech and song, as if she were reciting a liturgy that she knew from memory. As she continued to sing softly from within the confines of the netting, I began to sense again that I was in the presence of sacred beauty, its fragility already beginning to disappear in the early morning light. I thought of my marriage to Catherine and how desperately both of us had tried to find that nexus of something greater than ourselves, greater than even our children that would restore beauty to our relationship. The tragedy was that we both sensed its absence, but the chemistry of our marriage seemed incapable of bringing us both to that sacred space that for some couples is a timeless sincerity unfolding in layers of intimacy that are beyond words.

That was what Melissa had awakened within me. The strange, exotic intimations of Hebrew or Arabic somehow touched the center of my being that had been waiting patiently for years to be unlocked by the mystery of her voice. As dawn began to fill the room, I sat on the floor next to the bed allowing myself to breathe deeply, to be drawn into her ritual of adoration. With her lovely fingers, Melissa was carefully shaping the air around her as if she was suspended in water. It was as if she was actually touching a presence that was both sensory and religious.

Years later I learned that when those rare moments occur in our lives, when the veil of eternity is lifted even for a moment, our response should be to simply exist in that moment without attempting to prolong it with the hope of even greater insight. More importantly, I later came to realize that all life is sacred, from the fantastic to the mundane.

But I was not yet at that place. Instead my mind was racing ahead, attempting to remember meditation techniques that I learned in a class ten years earlier. As a result, I remained prostrate on the floor until I eventually fell asleep, awakened finally by the sound of Melissa in the shower and the bright rays of sun dancing on the wall opposite the bed.

I picked up the phone and ordered room service: soft boiled eggs, wheat toast with butter, and café au lait. When Melissa emerged from the bathroom she was fully dressed, and she looked incredibly rested and refreshed.

"You really didn't have to sleep on the floor. You must have been eaten alive by mosquitoes."

She was brushing out her long curly hair, and I watched as her fingers untangled a few of the stubborn knots. What I had witnessed hours earlier was beginning to seem like a dream. Over breakfast, Melissa seemed preoccupied with getting a message to her sister and brother-in-law who were staying in Livingstone on the Zambia side.

"They knew I was coming to The Victoria Falls Hotel for a drink; I should have called them last night. Trevor will be especially concerned."

"Call them from my phone."

"And say that I spent the night in your room?"

"Tell them you have decided to go with me by train to Harare."

"That's impossible. I'm heading to Cape Town tomorrow morning with Trevor and Kate. We'll be there for a week."

"Tell them you'll meet them in Cape Town next Saturday. That you've met an American businessman who has invited you on safari."

"Is that what we're doing? Going on safari?"

"We're going on an adventure. Besides, I want you to meet some of my diplomatic acquaintances in Harare. There's a reception on Wednesday evening."

As I mentioned the diplomatic reception I could tell that Melissa was suddenly interested.

"How did you know that I'm looking for a job?"

"I didn't know that until this very moment."

"I used to work at the French Embassy in Sydney arranging special events."

"Didn't know they celebrated Bastille Day in Australia."

"Don't be silly."

"Why did you leave?"

"I had to leave for my brother. He is in a messy situation in Bombay."

"What kind of messy situation?"

Melissa was staring at her half-eaten piece of toast. She was suddenly much more serious. Our conversation shifted from a playful romp to almost a dirge.

"He was arrested for smuggling drugs into India. For the last thirty-six months, he's been in jail and awaiting trial."

"Have you spoken to him?"

The rain had stopped and the room had that "leaving day" feel. It was the first awkward moment I had spent with Melissa, and I was searching for a way to change the subject, to restore the light-heartedness that had now exited the room.

"I've only spoken to Jonathan once since he was imprisoned. He called when he was first incarcerated, and our mother spoke to him last Christmas."

"Is your plan to go to Bombay?"

"My plan is to get the money we need to get him out."

I hesitated for a moment at her use of the plural pronoun. By "we" she must have meant her family or maybe just Kate and Trevor. I wondered how much they knew about the plight of Jonathan. As I knew from my own circumstances, sometimes families suppress embarrassing information, preferring avoidance over transparency. But aside from the family issue I was surprised by her directness: "My plan is to get the money." For a split second, the yellow caution lights came on, but I quickly dismissed them in favor of spending the next several hours with her as she began to rearrange her original plans.

By mid-morning, she had called her sister and Trevor, and they all agreed to meet the following Saturday in Cape Town. I spent the better part of the morning on the hotel terrace, reading Melissa's copy of Camus and sipping coffee while she had her luggage brought by car from the hotel in Livingstone. We spent an hour after lunch talking about philosophy and the first part of our itinerary to Harare—the overnight train from Victoria Falls to Bulawayo. Mostly, I wanted at all costs to avoid Teresa, even though I thought I owed her at least a cordial goodbye.

At 2:00 P.M. I hired a porter to take our bags from the hotel lobby to the train station, and of course while we were standing in the lobby, Teresa and Richard arrived at the main entrance to the hotel. Melissa must have noticed that I was visibly shaken at the sight of their arrival, and she instinctively slipped her arm through mine just as they appeared—now only twenty feet away. Richard looked mildly disgusted as Melissa and I stood directly in their path. He brought his right hand to his forehead as if to dismiss us with a tip of his hat, despite the fact that he was not wearing one. He wasn't going to speak to us, so the hat tip gesture served as a way for him to redirect to the other side of the lobby without having to address us in any way.

Teresa could have easily followed him and that would have been the end of it, but instead she chose to continue walking towards us. It has always amazed me how some women manage to keep their composure even in a sea of emotional conflict.

"Hello, Miss Samuel. James, how are you?"

The tone of Teresa's voice was almost identical to the "recalcitrant child" tone she had used almost exactly forty-eight hours earlier, and for a moment I thought she might try to convince both of us to check back into the hotel.

"Why don't the two of you join Richard and me and the children for dinner?"

Knowing almost nothing about my entanglement with Teresa, Melissa spoke up before I had a chance to respond.

"James and I are on the three o'clock train to Bulawayo, so dinner at the hotel is out of the question."

I didn't even want to look at Teresa to register her response, so instead I looked at Melissa, as if I were somewhat surprised to hear of our immediate departure.

"Are you walking to the station? If so, I'll walk with you. There are a few things I wanted to discuss with James before the two of you leave."

The three of us clumsily headed for the exit, and there was confusion at the front entrance about who should hold doors and who should go first. In the end we walked the short distance to the station with Teresa on my right and Melissa on my left. I felt like I was being escorted to the guillotine.

When we reached the station platform, Teresa did one of her faultless pivots and was directly in front of me.

"If Miss Samuel could just give us a moment, I wanted to say a heartfelt goodbye."

At that, Melissa continued walking down the platform and Teresa and I moved a few steps closer to the station house.

"Listen to me, James. To be kind I will only say that I am confused by your sudden alliance with Miss Samuel. And apparently you were hoping to avoid me all together before leaving Victoria Falls."

Neither of us spoke. I was waiting for the next segment, which would undoubtedly be the guilt and condemnation that I probably deserved.

Instead, Teresa took out a small piece of paper and talked as she wrote.

"Here's my private number at home in the States. You can call me at any time. I will always be there for you. Goodbye, James. I don't need to tell you that you're charming and attractive. But someday soon you'll have to stop being the great American boy-man and become the grownup you were actually meant to be."

Coming from Teresa, it was an incredibly gracious and profound goodbye, and as I followed her silhouette back up the hill, I could see the plumes of mist—the "smoke"—rising above the falls. As I paused, I had a quick flash of being reunited with her in this life or perhaps in the next. What I did not know, what I could not see until much later, was that I had chosen the wrong woman at Victoria Falls, and that choice would change the course of my life forever.

CHAPTER SIX

CHARLIE HEARD A KNOCK ON THE DOOR. FOR A MOMENT he thought it was Saturday morning and Ryan was knocking on their bedroom door. As the door opened, Charlie realized he was in Lake Louise, and the person entering the room was not Ryan, but Jenny.

"I brought you some coffee."

Jenny pulled up a chair and placed the coffee on the small bedside table.

"I need to apologize for last night. I completely overreacted."

Charlie reached for the coffee and sat up as the memory of Jenny's anger from the night before came rushing back.

"It's a lot to take in."

"But I was rude to you. Something that Papa would never be . . . especially to a stranger."

Jenny's quiet equilibrium had returned, and as Charlie sipped his coffee, he noticed that her left eyebrow had almost the exact peaked curvature of his own. It was at least one physical similarity that they shared, and he surmised that her remarkable green eyes must have been inherited from her mother.

"I already have a call in to Papa. I want to be sure he can come home tomorrow instead of Sunday. That way you could leave Sunday instead of today, and you two could meet and have a chance to talk."

Charlie's immediate thought was how could he possibly explain this newest delay to Heather. If he stayed until Sunday, he wouldn't be home until Monday evening at the earliest. Since he told her that he had already connected with James Monroe, what possible reason could he concoct for the delay?

"I'll need to call Heather and my office. No one will be happy, except for me, since I will have completed my Canadian mission."

"It's settled then. I'll convince Papa to return a day early, and we can all have dinner together tomorrow evening. Come down when you're ready."

After breakfast, Jenny continued to reassure Charlie that she could convince their father to return a day early. Charlie began to formulate how he would begin the conversation with Heather. Somehow he needed to convince her that his delayed return would be helpful to her, but every scenario he considered could not reconcile the reality that he would not be home by Sunday.

"We should go cross-country skiing."

Jenny had broken Charlie's silence, and they sat sipping coffee and looking at the streams of sunlight pouring in through the kitchen window.

"What's that?"

They both heard a vehicle out in the driveway and Charlie went to the window. A man was getting out of a large truck and inspecting Jenny's car.

"That must be the car guy from Banff who has already been here twice. I have had major electrical problems. No one seems to know how to fix it. I'd better go out there and find out if he is making any progress."

Despite only having on her Chinese robe, Jenny slipped on a pair of boots, grabbed her car keys, and headed out the door. Charlie could see her handing the man the keys, and he was surprised that they were still in conversation almost ten minutes later.

As Charlie headed up the stairs to his room, he heard the chime ring of Jenny's phone.

"Might be James calling her back," Charlie thought, and he grabbed the phone from the kitchen counter and headed out to the driveway. By the time he reached the door, the ringing had stopped, and when he handed Jenny the phone, the man was in the driver's seat, starting and restarting the car.

"He thinks the relay is bad, but I just had the relay replaced last year."

"Electrical problems can be endless. Someone called; I thought it might be James."

"That's not Papa's number. It's from the States. Maybe Heather got my number?"

Jenny meant it to be playful, but Charlie's response was more a shrug than a shared laugh. He headed back inside, and a few minutes later, he heard the truck start up in the driveway.

"Let's go cross-country skiing. It's way too nice to stay inside." Jenny was at the bottom of the stairs, and at the sound of her voice, Charlie emerged from his room.

"Did he fix your car?"

"He's coming back this afternoon with a new relay. I feel like I'm in relay hell."

"What size are your dad's cross-country ski boots?"

"Size ten. I bought him new ones for Christmas."

Since Charlie was a size ten, he knew that his last excuse for not cross-country skiing had just evaporated. He was supposed to be heading home, but instead he would spend the afternoon with Jenny on cross-country ski trails near Banff National Park.

"We'll take the Lake Moraine trail. Moraine Lake has the bluest water you've ever seen."

As they prepared to head out, Charlie noticed that Jenny had a quick fifteen-minute routine that allowed her to be on the trail at a moment's notice. As he was still getting on his boots, she was already in the driveway, arranging her small backpack and tucking her hair into her woolen hat.

As they headed toward the trail, Jenny glided effortlessly along, moving in smooth strides as they approached the trailhead. It had been years since Charlie had gone cross-country skiing, and so he was amazed at how quickly he remembered the skating motion that was needed to navigate small rises and the heel-toe action needed to cross level or downhill terrain.

By the time they reached the first trail marker, it was a little before noon and the sky was beginning to gray over, portending an afternoon snow. They stopped briefly for a water break, and as they were shoving off, Charlie's cell phone began its rendition of "Sweet Melissa." Charlie glanced at his phone. It was Heather.

"Do you need to answer that?"

"My office," Charlie lied. "If I answer it, my afternoon will be completely ruined."

"Oh my God, where's my phone?"

Jenny checked every pocket and even rifled through her backpack.

"You must have left it in the kitchen; why do you need it?"

"All of our plans for Papa to come home tomorrow depend on us talking to him today. I better go back for it."

"Didn't you leave him a message?"

"Papa doesn't listen to his messages."

"So should we both go back?"

"No, I'll go back and either catch up or I'll go around the other side and meet you where the trail goes by the lake."

"Is the trail completely marked?"

"The trail is incredibly well marked. You need to see the lake—it's worth the effort of the five-mile loop."

At that Jenny backed up a few feet and changed direction.

"You'll be fine, Charlie. See you in about forty minutes. I won't be long."

Charlie watched as Jenny disappeared back down the trail. She was already skiing much faster than before, and her promise to either catch up or meet him at the next trailhead seemed more reasonable. He continued to the next marker, and as he began to catch glimpses of the lake, it began to snow. At one point on the trail there was a small lookout, and Charlie surmised that he was probably as close to the lake as the trail would permit. Thinking that Jenny would appear from one direction or the other in a matter of minutes, he remained at the lookout and took in the panoramic view of the lake surrounded by peaks that reminded him of pictures he had seen of Switzerland.

The only sound was the crystals of snow falling in the pine branches, and Charlie realized that he hadn't experienced this depth of natural solitude since his teenage years at his grandparents' camp in northern Michigan. His life now was one of constant movement and commotion. His daily mantra was if he hoped to survive, he needed to keep moving.

Somehow Jenny (and perhaps his father) had found a different existence out here in the Pacific Northwest. They both worked off and on at the crisis house in Vancouver, but much of their time was spent here in Lake Louise. Their lives were simple, but intentional. He couldn't imagine how they got by financially, and for a brief moment it dawned on him that perhaps his mother might have shared some of her limited wealth whenever she intuitively sensed that James was in need. He had no idea if Teresa and his father had stayed in touch after their meeting in Africa, but her knowing that James was his real father would have been a strong incentive.

Charlie had been standing there for at least ten minutes and the snow was intensifying. He thought about returning on the same path he had just traversed, but he knew Jenny would be disappointed if he didn't do the full loop. "Besides," he thought, "by continuing on around, I'll probably encounter her coming from the other direction."

With the intensifying snow, the two and a half miles that would bring him back to the first trailhead became increasingly more challenging. Jenny had failed to tell him that mile four was a series of small hills, and at one point he removed his skis and traversed one of the steepest inclines on foot.

He now assumed that Jenny was behind him and, with her expert technique, would overtake him at any moment. At one point he thought he heard her screaming, and he stopped to listen. He was engulfed in the silence of the forest, and because his hands and feet were already numb from the cold, he decided to press on, already anticipating the warmth of the fire and the inevitable cups of tea that she would prepare upon their return. He finally reached the trailhead and mustered his last bit of strength to traverse the last two hundred yards back to the house.

As he came into the clearing that he considered to be their very large front yard, he heard Jenny's car running, and as he glided into the driveway, he saw her cross-country skis standing upright next to the front door.

"She must have decided not to come," he thought. "Probably had something to do with James's homecoming."

As he removed his skis and placed them carefully next to hers, he half expected to see her in the doorway, apologetic about her decision not to rejoin him. Instead, there was only the sound of the falling snow.

"Hello, anybody home?" Charlie thought of his similar salutation when he had first arrived.

Opening the door, he glanced over at the fire and noticed that it was almost out. Instinctively he placed two logs on the coals and then called up from the bottom of the stairs.

"Jenny, are you up there?"

His own voice echoed in the second-floor hallway. He checked her bedroom, the bathroom, the kitchen, and the backyard. She wasn't there.

Charlie sat down in front of the fire and tried to sort out a logical explanation. He didn't even have her cell number. He checked his bedroom and the front closet on the off chance that she might have gone snowshoeing. All the snowshoes were tucked carefully away. He was trying to remain rational, but the rational explanations for her sudden disappearance were down to two or three possibilities—none of them very reasonable.

"She probably has multiple pairs of Nordic skis," he thought. "She may have decided to switch skis when she returned because of a faulty binding."

He realized the implausibility of that explanation, but as he sat longer next to the fire, it grew in plausibility, and for several moments Charlie was sure that she was still out on the trail and would appear at any minute. Besides, he couldn't say for sure whether the skis next to the front door were there or not there when they left on the trail.

As the sun began to set and the fire became the only light source in the room, Charlie turned on the same table lamps from the night before, and for a moment the friendly atmosphere of the living room seemed to dispel her absence; then, a few seconds later, it made it worse. He had abandoned the "still on the trail" theory and now was convincing himself that she must have decided to walk the three or four miles to the village.

Suddenly he remembered that her car had been running when he had returned. He put on his coat and boots and headed out to investigate. It was nearly completely dark, but he climbed into the driver's seat and turned off the ignition. The engine ground to a halt. He opened the door, and as he did something next to the door jamb fell into the snow. At first he thought it was just a paper receipt, but it wasn't. It was Jenny's white porcelain hair clip.

Charlie sat there in disbelief. When they had stopped for water earlier that afternoon, she had removed her woolen hat for just a moment. Charlie remembered thinking how perfect it was that Jenny wore her hair clip even for trail skiing. Now he just sat there staring at it, and for the first time he allowed himself to imagine the unimaginable: the repair guy in the truck.

So many thoughts came rushing into his head that for a few minutes he continued to sit in the driver's seat with the car door open, the snow quietly covering his left arm and leg until he mechanically headed back into the house, still clutching the clip.

At home he would have called 911 and been told that he could not file a missing person's report until the person was missing for twenty-four hours (or maybe forty-eight hours). He couldn't remember. But this situation had too many moving parts. Was it possible that Jenny had contacted their father and for some reason she had to rush to Vancouver? Maybe she considered taking her car, and then, thinking better of it, borrowed a car from a neighbor? But she would have left a note. And Charlie had already checked. There wasn't a note, and he had looked everywhere.

He now considered his own position. He was in Alberta, Canada. He had spent the night in the house alone with Jenny. He was there on a hunch that her father was also his father, but he actually didn't know for sure. He wondered about his legal rights as an American citizen in Canada. If Jenny was missing and later presumed dead, he would surely be the prime suspect.

He paused as the unthinkable began to surface. The only people who knew he was in Lake Louise were Jenny, Heather, and the repair guy in the truck. And did the truck guy actually see him? After all, the mechanic had been in the driver's seat when Charlie had come outside with Jenny's phone. Wasn't he preoccupied with the ignition switch?

If he just got in his car and drove home, would anyone be able to put all of those pieces together? Charlie thought of his fingerprints all over the house—including the bathtub—and for a moment he wondered if Canada and the United States shared fingerprint information. And there was the message that Jenny had left on James's phone. She had mentioned that Charlie was the son of a good friend from Africa. James would remember Teresa Benjamin, and Charlie would be arrested in Winnetka in a matter of weeks.

The other unknown was the guy in the truck. If he did abduct Jenny, was he smart enough to think that Charlie could be his alibi? Was he smart enough to have written down Charlie's license plate number either that morning or when he returned in the afternoon? It was entirely possible that the mechanic had been completely undone by her lovely legs, her green eyes, and the openness of her smile. He could have formulated his plan that morning and by chance his return and her return to the house had happened to coincide. All of these variables rushed in on him, and he began to think of how unassuming it had been for Jenny to stand in her driveway at ten o'clock in the morning, wearing only boots and her robe.

It was now almost 6:00 P.M., and Charlie realized that his only option was to stay another night. He didn't have his father's number in Vancouver. Jenny (and her phone) were gone. His one task for the evening was to call Heather, and he had already decided that he would have to tell her the truth.

As he dialed her number, his one hope was voicemail. Instead, in typical Heather style, she answered in mid-conversation.

"Please tell me you are already halfway home."

"Hi honey, I'm actually still in Lake Louise."

"Your office called here three times today. According to Craig, you aren't answering your phone or responding to email. Are you trying to get fired?"

"I'm in a somewhat messy situation here. Something unexpected has happened."

"Did your father die?"

"Nothing like that. It involves a missing person."

"A friend of your father's is missing?"

Charlie could tell that Heather was multitasking as she often did on the phone, probably cleaning up the kitchen or folding laundry and only half listening to his replies. Her real intention was to find the opportune moment in the conversation to assert her own agenda and be sure that he would be home by noon on Sunday.

"It's actually his daughter. My half sister."

"Where does she live?"

"She also lives here in Lake Louise."

"Can't your father handle this? Why do you have to also be there?"

"Look Heather, I wasn't completely honest with you last night. I stayed here last night with my half sister; I haven't actually met my father."

"What?"

He could visualize Heather now drying her hands or pulling her hair away from her face as she actually began to focus on what he was saying.

"James Monroe is in Vancouver. We were expecting him to be here tomorrow."

Charlie could tell that Heather was recalibrating her responses, attempting to zero in on his fault line.

"Is your half sister married?"

"She never married, which is odd."

As soon as he said "which is odd" he regretted using that phrase.

"Why is it odd? How old is she?"

"Maybe late forties, early fifties."

"Is it odd that she's not married because she's so attractive?"

Heather had this ability to cut through to the truth that often elevated her role to that of prosecuting attorney. When she assumed this role, Charlie usually reverted to a defensive posture that only encouraged more questions.

"So you spent last night somewhere in Canada with an attractive woman in her late forties who has never been married?"

The way Heather said it, it sounded so incriminating. It occurred to Charlie that if he weren't careful, she would somehow find out about his being in the bathroom while Jenny was in the bathtub. A part of him realized that she would eventually find that out as well.

"Did you sleep with her?"

With truth on his side, he was suddenly able to sound much more indignant.

"Of course I didn't sleep with her; she's my half sister."

"And now she's your half sister who is also a missing person? I don't get it."

"I don't get it" was one of Heather's favorite taglines. She could sprinkle it into random remarks to add both incredulity and disdain.

"I'm pretty sure she was abducted by an auto mechanic."

As he said it, Charlie was aware of how ridiculous it sounded, and he had a premonition that someone in law enforcement might have the same reaction. For Heather it was the perfect transition to sarcasm, which was another weapon in her prosecutorial toolbox.

"Was the mechanic an alien? Was your half sister abducted by aliens?"

In any other circumstance, Charlie's response would have been laughter, but the stark reality of his situation forced him to be silent. Heather pressed on.

"Where were you when the abduction took place? Was it at night?"

Charlie hesitated. Heather was clearly on a roll, and he was quickly losing all credibility. Better at this point to return to the facts.

"We went cross-country skiing." Charlie paused. He couldn't even begin to imagine how she would react to that image. But he continued. "We went cross-country skiing, and Jenny went back to the house to get her phone. When I returned an hour later, she was gone."

"She's probably at a girlfriend's house." Heather was picturing the neighborhoods of Winnetka where, despite the affluence, the houses are fairly close together. "She's been away four or five hours and you assume she's been abducted? She's there, Charlie; she's in the neighborhood. And even if she doesn't come home tonight, she's an adult. She has her own private life. Leave her a note, pack up the car and come home."

The way Heather said it, it sounded so easy. For a second, Charlie thought of telling her about the hairclip and the Chinese robe Jenny was wearing in the driveway.

Instead he decided to agree with Heather, to allow her to envision him packing up the car and leaving Canada. He had no idea how he would explain things to her tomorrow evening or three days from now when he was still in Lake Louise. And so, as he had done on previous occasions with Heather, he lied.

"Maybe you're right. I'll leave Jenny a note, pack up my things, and head out this evening. If all goes well, I'll be home by midday on Sunday."

He paused to give her the satisfaction that she relished when she had her own way.

"Goodnight, Heather."

"Goodnight, Charlie. Ryan will be excited that you'll be here for his tournament. Drive safely."

Charlie hit the "end call" button on his phone, poured himself a whiskey, and sat by the fire. He had heard Jenny scream when he was on mile four of the trail, and now he knew that she had been screaming in desperation. He imagined the mechanic inviting her to sit in the driver's seat, to try out the new ignition box, and he saw him grabbing her by the neck and hair, dragging her from her car to his truck as she cried out, screaming for help.

He wondered if, at that very moment, she was being abused or tortured. It also occurred to him that she might already be dead.

Tomorrow morning he would have to find a way to get in touch with his father in Vancouver. He would be talking to him for the first time and he would be calling to tell him that his son had been found, but that his daughter, the love of his life, was now lost.

CHAPTER SEVEN

HAVING NOW SURVIVED MY EXTENDED GOODBYE TO Teresa, I headed to the other end of the platform, where Melissa was already engaged in a lively conversation with two porters.

"They are saying that the two-berth cabins won't be available for an hour, so they are inviting us to sit in the first-class lounge car for the first part of the trip."

She seemed mildly annoyed that our accommodation was not yet ready, and I assured her that the first class-lounge would undoubtedly be even more comfortable than our cabin. As it turned out, the lounge car was almost empty, and the porter suggested that we sit on the south-facing side to be able to see the exotic wildlife as we passed through Hwange National Park. We each ended up having a full bench to ourselves, and we were facing one another. Exotic wildlife to my right and a full view of Melissa—I thought about how I might convince her to stay here for more than an hour.

Perhaps aware that Melissa had been somewhat annoyed about the delay of our cabin, the porter assigned to our car brought us blankets and hot tea and even gave us a brochure explaining what wildlife we might expect to see at the western end of Hwange. All in all it was very civilized, and despite what I considered to be the slow speed of the train—we were only going forty-five mph—our speed would be perfect for viewing the park's wildlife. One of the legacies of British colonial rule is the excellent rail system in Zimbabwe, and it looks and runs much as it did when the British departed fourteen years ago in 1980.

In the early days of RR (Rhodesia Railways) you could take the train all the way from Victoria Falls to the Indian Ocean. What is now Mozambique had once been Portuguese East Africa, and Portuguese explorers in the sixteenth century may have navigated their way from where the Zambezi reaches the Indian Ocean all the way back upstream to Victoria Falls—a distance of over one thousand miles. Even though David Livingstone is credited with being the first European to see the falls in 1855, Portuguese explorers may well have preceded him by three centuries.

Melissa sat across from me sipping tea and reading a copy of Beyond Good and Evil by Friedrich Nietzsche. I now surmised that the weight of her suitcase was due to at least ten books, which she faithfully carried with her wherever she went. Just that she read philosophy elevated my estimation of her basic goodness immeasurably and perpetuated my theory of her as somewhat of a goddess as evidenced by her apotheosis at the Devil's Pool and her quiet recitation of an ancient Hebrew liturgy as she slept last evening in my bed. She embodied a sacred beauty that I had longed for all of my life, and now I was about to spend thirteen hours with her on an overnight train to Bulawayo.

As the porter was replenishing our tea and informing us of the additional wait time for our cabin, I noticed a large herd of springbok seemingly running to keep up with the train. The vastness of the plain in this part of the park was a little overwhelming and the sun was already casting long shadows over the veld that made the distance of the herd from the train tracks difficult to calculate. I could not fully see the part of the herd still trailing behind, but there must have been thousands of springbok in the distance.

Melissa glanced out at them off and on, but her current fixation was on Nietzsche. She had removed her shoes and tucked her legs up under her so that her skirt, which was mid-calf length, was drawn up to almost her knees. At one point she stretched out both of her legs and placed them between my own. As the train occasionally jostled back and forth, the nylon of her stockings gently touched my legs. I pretended to be fully engrossed in the spectacle of wildlife to my right, but my true fascination was with the casual flirtation occurring just inches away. Could it be possible that she was unaware of the electrifying effect she was having on me? As if to answer my unspoken question, she pulled both of her legs back to their tucked position and carefully placed a bookmark in Nietzsche.

"Where's the porter? Our cabin must be ready by now."

The porter was not in the lounge car, so I embarked on what turned out to be a three-car search for the man who had originally promised only a one-hour delay. When I finally found him, he could see in my eyes that I was becoming impatient.

"Your cabin is ready, sir. Because of your wait, we gave you the best two-berth cabin on the train. Your water is hot and your beds are already made."

I went back to retrieve Melissa. We followed the porter through several sleeper cars and finally arrived at our two-berth cabin. As promised, it was nicer than we had expected.

"This is one of the 1952 wood-paneled cabins built in Gloucester, England. Best on the train."

Even though we had waited nearly two hours, I tipped him generously for giving us what was essentially an upgrade, and he promised to return later on to prepare the cabin for the night.

"Why did you tip him?" Melissa's question took me off guard.

"I always tip porters on a train."

"Then you tipped him for his inefficiency."

"It wasn't his fault our cabin wasn't ready."

"It was someone's fault. He said one hour and it was really two hours."

I couldn't believe that Melissa was still arguing about the tip.

"We weren't exactly roughing it in the lounge car."

"I'm just saying that if you tip people for their inefficiency, they will do the same thing tomorrow."

"Maybe you've been reading too much Nietzsche."

"Nietzsche would say that we all should aspire to greatness, and pity will dissipate that desire."

"I don't think of my tip as an act of pity."

"All I'm saying is that if we enable weakness, there will be no growth."

I thought of those passengers who could not afford a sleeper car and who would attempt to sleep upright in their seats for the entire night, but I also sensed that we were moving to that point in the argument where we were arguing over words more than ideas. Instead of prolonging it, I chose to simply acquiesce.

"You have a point. We don't want to encourage inefficiency."

Melissa knew that I was slightly mocking her earlier point, but she too decided it had gone far enough. Months later I would look back on this conversation and realize that it had an import that I could only fully appreciate in retrospect.

Our small disagreement had the potential to ruin (or at least dampen) the eleven hours remaining on the journey, but I was so infatuated with the idea that my lifelong quest for a union of the sacred and the beautiful had finally been realized, that I began working to get back to that earlier revelation. I knew that we had moved one step away from the perfection I had perceived in her even an hour before, but I was not ready to admit that she was something less than a goddess.

Dinner would be pivotal. Somehow in the enjoyment of good food and wine in the dining car, I hoped we would reconnect on the same wavelength we had enjoyed at The Victoria Falls Hotel. Melissa insisted at dinner that I review with her the names of those who would attend the Wednesday reception in Harare. I did so willingly, knowing that she would be buoyed by the array of local celebrities and dignitaries.

"Who will be there from the French consulate in Harare?"

She was particularly interested in any French diplomats and journalists, since (as was later confirmed at the reception) she spoke fluent French.

"The most colorful French diplomat I know is Pierre Jonquin. He worked for the French Consulate-General in Cairo, and he has held several posts in sub-Saharan countries, including Kenya and Zimbabwe. He knows almost every French national in the region. He will probably know some of your buddies from the French Embassy in Sydney."

I knew that the more I talked about Wednesday evening, the more relaxed Melissa would become. She had sacrificed quite a bit to be on this trip, but the payoff in her mind would be the diplomatic reception. I sensed that she knew that she only needed a few hours at a diplomatic cocktail party and she could land a job. I was happy to provide that venue, but in the interim I wanted our relationship to progress from friendship to something more.

At dessert I began to anticipate how we might handle the close quarters of a double berth cabin, and as we were talking over coffee, our porter appeared to tell us he had opened our screen and that there were fresh sheets on the bed. I thought about tipping him, but I didn't want to return to the tipping conversation just as we were beginning to enjoy the normalcy of our friendship.

Melissa took my hand and we made our way past five or six sleeping cars until we reached our cabin. The porter had left the light on over the sink, and as we entered, Melissa reached up and pulled the small chain, leaving the room almost in complete darkness. I sat down on the bed and she quietly exited to use the small bathroom down the corridor.

When she returned, she locked the door and began to undress. I was still fully dressed, but in the small space, I was reclined and facing her. She removed her skirt and blouse and carefully folded them and placed them on the small table next to the sink. She slipped off her bracelet and earrings, put them in her shoe, and then pulled back the sheet and small blanket on her side. It was then that I noticed the hairbrush in her left hand.

As she sat up, she pulled the sheet up to her waist and carefully removed her bra and placed it on the small shelf next to her. She was now almost completely naked, and to increase the sheer sensuality of the moment, she began to brush out her hair. In the darkened cabin, the static electricity from her hair created small sparks of light and added to the mystery that she had first awakened in me when she flashed a smile in my direction at the Devil's Pool.

Without any further hesitation, I found my way to the cabin door, slipped out into the corridor and found the bathroom. When I returned to the cabin, I found Melissa still sitting up in bed, brushing her hair.

Not bothering to be nearly as fastidious as she had been, I took off my clothes and slipped into bed beside her.

"Will you brush my hair?"

Her question was a very quiet one, and as she handed me the brush, I felt like I was entering a place of sacred mystery. The whole mood of the room was accentuated by the slight swaying back and forth of the car and the hypnotic sound of the wheels crossing the seams in the tracks.

We were on the eastern end of Hwange National Park and somewhere in the darkness just south of the train's trajectory were zebra, elephant, giraffe, and even lion, and I imagined both their beauty and their instinct for survival which haunted the veld under the cover of night.

Melissa's hair was long, and it had curls at the ends. Through some experimenting, I discovered that if I used my left hand to hold up a section of hair while brushing with my right, it allowed me to actually brush her hair instead of simply pulling at it. Using this same method I was able to begin at her neckline and I allowed the soft bristles to lightly touch her neck as I brushed up and underneath the thickness of her curls.

She swung her body around so that she was seated cross-legged and facing away from me. She then extended both arms behind her so that her neck was extended back while her hair fell right in front of me. I supported her neck with one hand and with the other continued the brushing technique I had perfected just a moment before.

Soon we both became exhausted in this position and she simply rested her head on my calf as I stroked her hair until she fell asleep. I became aware that this was the more intimate version of the Selene-Endymion narrative, and I was again happy to watch over her as she slept. I thought more about the role gender plays in establishing intimacy. I had learned that gender fluidity in relationships between men and women allows for greater creativity, as both sides yearn to fully express their love and care. As a man I was not afraid of this gender role-play, since it allowed me to more fully express my vulnerability. I am not effeminate, and I value my masculine identity, but true masculinity means you are secure enough to express a full range of sensuality and emotion, knowing that to do so allows your partner the freedom to do the same. I was attracted to Melissa because of her beauty and her athleticism, but more than that she was able to express divine mystery through a spirituality that was embedded in her subconscious. Some men might ignore this mysterious side of her; for me it was the nexus that drew me near.

I must have briefly fallen asleep, because when I awakened, I was lying back and Melissa had shifted so that her body lay next to mine and her head was now resting on my shoulder. As she slept,

I could feel her warm breath on my neck and her lovely tresses of hair lying across my chest. The movement of the train meant that our bodies moved together back and forth as we moved through the night. It was similar to sleeping close to someone at sea.

Since my divorce I had experienced an undercurrent of restlessness that had become a subconscious nemesis to finding intimacy. It was as if my reserve of authentic emotion had been irrevocably depleted, so that I was often unable to feel anything. Some people mistook this for a manly stoicism—a barrier that successfully separated my head from my heart. Essentially, I had become a person longing for intimacy who was incapable of sustaining it for any length of time.

I like my job as a researcher and economist for the Bank, but I liked it for the wrong reasons. Because I was assigned to sub-Saharan Africa, I was traveling almost six months out of the year. And travel matched my internal disposition on many different levels. Because of travel, I was often not in any one place long enough to form significant relationships. Instead, I fulfilled unrequited longings of other people—mostly women—who would shape me into their unfulfilled dream, even though I was not the person they may have fantasized me to be.

Travel also allowed me to live continually in the future without overthinking the present. For example, even though we were still in Zimbabwe, I was already thinking ahead to next week's trip to Nairobi—where I would stay, who I would have dinner with, etc.

Lying next to Melissa, traveling through the night to Bulawayo, I focused on treasuring every moment, and so I allowed the intimacy of the two of us sleeping together to begin to dispel the restlessness, to become the sedative that would quiet my heart. Her soft breathing was an intoxication, a way for me to believe again that I was fully connected to the rest of humanity, that I was desirable and authentic and capable of love. I longed for that authenticity, for that identity that would allow me to define myself through small acts of kindness. A woman's love and tenderness seemed to be the highest expression of that authenticity, but there were times when I wondered whether that might also be a trompe l'oeil, a deception designed to keep us from discovering a more authentic love than we could possibly imagine, one that was impervious to the vagaries of chance and misfortune—a love so real and intense that we might be lost in it forever.

At around 6:00 A.M. the porter knocked on our door to deliver both coffee and tea. He must have become accustomed to being greeted by travelers who were just waking up, as he seemed unfazed when I opened the door wearing only boxers.

With Melissa still asleep, I tipped him and he promised to return within thirty minutes with fried egg sandwiches. The view of the sunrise from our cabin window was spectacular, and as I sipped coffee and waited for Melissa to stir, I reviewed the AFREA paperwork that I had received by fax the day before at the hotel. I was scheduled to have lunch in Nairobi a week from Tuesday with a former government official from the Maharashtra State in India. I assumed it had to do with their request for Bank assistance with the road construction project already underway in Bombay. The Indian government always seemed to be mired in paperwork, so I wasn't surprised that the negotiations were still going on five years after the initial proposal.

When the porter arrived with our breakfast, Melissa stirred and made a low moan, indicating both her satisfaction with a good night's sleep and her acknowledgement that her hunger for toast and coffee now obliged her to at least sit up in bed. She gathered the sheets around her and pulled back her hair behind both ears.

"I think I fell asleep after that fabulous hair brushing session. You must have brushed women's hair before. You're somewhat of an expert."

I wondered if she was secretly curious as to why the hair brushing hadn't led to even more intimate contact, but we both knew that prolonged anticipation in a relationship is not a bad thing, since the longing for consummation is often more emotionally intense than the event itself. I knew that there would be other opportunities—even that evening—to be intimate, and I continued to believe that there was a sanctity about her that I was anxious not to violate.

Being next to her for most of the night was in perfect alignment with the trust factor that we all want to experience before giving ourselves over completely to another person. Otherwise, the physical act itself eclipses the emotional bonding that brings two people together in a union that is both timeless and sacrosanct. It had not been that way with Teresa, but in retrospect, despite the tawdry implications, there had been an innocence and an inevitability to that evening that affected both of us for decades to come.

"When do we arrive in Bulawayo?"

Melissa was already at the sink, still partially naked and giving herself a sponge bath. I thought about offering to help, but our moment for intimacy had already passed, and Melissa was readying herself for the day.

"The porter said 8:00 A.M. I know you don't trust him to keep his word, but he has little control over the speed of the train."

Melissa chose to ignore more porter discussions.

"Is there a dress shop in Bulawayo? I need a dress for Wednesday's reception."

I imagined spending the morning watching Melissa trying on cocktail dresses, and I wondered if in addition to accommodation at the Bulawayo Club, Melissa would ask me to pay for her dress. She had made it clear she was job hunting, so she might be short on cash.

"We can ask at the Club. I'm sure they will know a shop. It would be a privilege to join you as you try on dresses."

At Melissa's suggestion we packed up our cabin and headed to the lounge car for the final hour of the trip. Seeing a Harare newspaper on the seat next to mine, I was reminded that we would be on the train again tomorrow for the thirteen-hour trip to Harare.

I had only been to the Bulawayo Club one other time, but I was looking forward to the sumptuous paneled interior and the small bar decorated with pictures of colonial scions such as Cecil Rhodes and Ian Smith. The Club was incorporated in 1895 as a gentlemen's club, and it remains along with The Victoria Falls Hotel and the Meikles Hotel in Harare as one of the last surviving bastions of Rhodesian colonial history. There is a billiards room, but the preferred game is snooker, which is played on a billiards table but with completely different rules. Like The Victoria Falls Hotel and Meikles, the Bulawayo Club is a daily destination for Bulawayo's most prominent citizens, and when you enter you see the local gentry reading newspapers and having tea or, later in the day, a drink.

As it turned out, our train arrived in Bulawayo closer to 9:00, and by the time we got a cab to transport us and our luggage the ten blocks to the Club, it was closer to 10:00. There had been many attractive women staying at The Victoria Falls Hotel, but Bulawayo was not a destination town as much as a stop on the way to Victoria Falls or Harare. So I was a little taken aback by the admiring glances that Melissa received as we entered the lobby of the Club, and I quickly calculated that the wisest tact to take would be to register as husband and wife.

"I have a reservation."

The desk clerk was busy counting cash, probably from their liquor sales of the night before.

"What is the name, sir?"

"Monroe, James Monroe."

"For one person?"

"Actually, my wife has joined me, so there are two of us."

"Have you stayed here before?"

"One time, probably two years ago."

"You are booked into a premium room, but since it is for Sunday evening I can upgrade you to an executive suite."

I could tell Melissa was becoming impatient. The desk clerk in her mind was becoming inefficient and too talkative. I decided to calm her.

"Is there a dress shop in town?"

It was the wrong thing to ask. It seemed to throw him off completely.

"Let me give you your room key, and I'll find the manager."

He returned in a few minutes and introduced us to a stentorian-looking man in his fifties who had glasses and a small mustache.

"How can I help you?"

"My wife and I are just staying one night, and we are looking for a dress shop—somewhere that sells evening clothes."

"The only shop like that is Maxine's, but they are closed on Sundays."

"It's fine, James," said Melissa, "We can find a dress in Harare."

I realized that there was a part of me that wanted to be heroic for her—to take an impossible situation and somehow solve it.

"Is that our only alternative?"

The manager hesitated.

"They did open the shop on Sunday afternoon a few months ago, but it was for a matron of honor whose luggage had been lost at the Harare airport. I could give them a call. In the meantime, why don't you get settled in your room, and I'll let you know either way."

I was fully expecting that he would not be able to find the owner, and we would have to rush around on Tuesday afternoon or Wednesday morning to find Melissa a dress. Instead, he called our room almost immediately with the news that we could meet the owner there at 3:00 P.M.

When I hung up the phone and told Melissa the good news, she walked across the room, put her hand on the back of my neck, and gave me a longer-than-friendship kiss on the mouth. It was the first time we had kissed, and in those few seconds, as her tongue briefly touched the outside of my lips, I sensed that to journey into the world of her sensuality would be both ecstatically erotic and potentially dangerous. Like everything else about Melissa, her sexuality had an intensity about it that was impossibly attractive yet somehow also forbidden, as if the risk of falling for her might ultimately result in a point of no return.

Maxine's dress shop was only a few blocks from the Bulawayo Club, so after lunch and a nap, we walked there, arriving a few minutes early. The front door was open, and as we entered, a chime announced our arrival. A well-dressed woman, probably in her mid-fifties (undoubtedly Maxine herself), emerged from the recesses of the shop, and as soon as she greeted us, I detected a European accent, probably Czech or Bulgarian.

"You must be Mr. and Mrs. Monroe."

I loved the idea of people addressing Melissa as my wife.

"Tell me the occasion for the dress. Is the event this evening?"

I wasn't sure what the concierge at the Club might have said about the urgency of opening the shop on Sunday, so I quickly elevated the importance of Wednesday's reception.

"Mrs. Monroe and I have been invited to a diplomatic reception in Harare. This will be our only opportunity to buy a dress."

I intentionally left out the Wednesday timeframe, and before I had a chance to say more, Maxine had again disappeared to the back of the store, and she re-emerged in about five minutes, wheeling a rack of elegant dresses.

"I'm guessing you're a size six, and you're in luck. I have some lovely sixes that will make Mrs. Monroe the envy of every woman in the room."

I sat off to the side, content to spend the next forty-five minutes watching Melissa try on some of Maxine's prized collection. All of them looked terrific on her, but in the end she chose a black velvet, just-below-the-knee evening dress with a sheer neckline that complimented her lovely neck and shoulders. It made her look sophisticated and slightly provocative, and as I paid Maxine in cash, I thought of how proud I would be to have her at my side on Wednesday evening. As we headed out the door, Melissa paused our progress and kissed me on the cheek.

"Thank you, James. What a lovely gift."

Although there were numerous restaurant choices for dinner, we decided instead to stay at the Club, and we both agreed that an early night would probably be wise, as we had another lengthy train ride to Harare the next day.

After dinner we decamped to the famous Bulawayo Club bar and billiard room for an after-dinner drink, and when we arrived there were two men who had left their brandy snifters at the bar so that they could focus completely on their game of snooker.

Melissa wandered over to the snooker table while I ordered drinks, and in a few minutes she had engaged one of the men in conversation.

"Didn't know I would find a fellow Aussie in the hinterlands of Zimbabwe!"

The man addressing Melissa had reddish-brown hair, and I guessed he was in his mid-fifties. He was muscular and athletic looking, and he looked like he could easily snap the snooker stick if he became agitated due to a poor shot.

I handed Melissa her drink, and I noticed that she was intently watching the strategic shots of both players.

"Do you know the rules of this game?"

My question was to Melissa, but it was loud enough for both men to hear. They looked over at me with a disdain that I had experienced before when dealing with citizens of the Commonwealth.

"I grew up playing snooker in Melbourne. I was actually school champion one year at St. Margaret's."

"Did I hear Melbourne?"

The man with reddish-brown hair was now looking at Melissa.

"I was school champion two years running."

"That's impressive. We didn't even have a snooker table at Carey Baptist."

"You went to Carey Baptist Grammar School?"

"I'm sorry to say that I was there for six years. Wasn't the school's fault. I was more interested in sport than studies."

At this Melissa moved closer to the table.

"I haven't played snooker in ten years, but I would love to take on the winner."

Both men looked at each other, and I could see the skepticism in their eyes. It was one thing for a woman to have a drink at the bar, but for a woman to challenge a man to a game of snooker at the Bulawayo Club was undoubtedly a first.

"Sure, you can play the winner, but we still have another frame after this one, so it may be awhile. By the way, I'm Marcus Finch, and my buddy here is John Langford."

Melissa extended her hand.

"I'm Melissa Monroe and this is my husband, James Monroe."

We all shook hands across the table, and I noticed that Marcus held Melissa's hand just a second or two longer than what would be considered a normal greeting. Melissa and I returned to the bar, and as we sat facing the snooker table Melissa attempted to explain the snooker rules.

"Different colored balls have different points. If you pot a colored ball, it must be followed by a red ball pot. The strategy is to avoid fouls and to amass as many points as possible in a frame."

I thought about the enormous mahogany four-poster bed in our executive suite. Tomorrow evening would be another double berth on the train, and although our train cabin was comfortable, train sleeping could not compete with the space and amenities of the Bulawayo Club. I decided to try to convince Melissa to forego the snooker challenge.

"Instead of having another drink, why don't we head up to the room?"

Melissa continued to stare at the table, and she took another sip of brandy.

"I can't allow these Aussies to think they've scared me off."

"Since we've barely met them, does it really matter?"

If anything, my questioning was making her more firmly entrenched.

"I can't let them think that a St. Margaret's girl would walk away from a challenge."

I decided to revert to a little sarcasm.

"We wouldn't want your Melbourne grammar school to be disgraced in Bulawayo."

But Melissa could not be humored, and I could hear her next suggestion before the words were delivered.

"Why don't you go on up and I'll join you in less than an hour?"

If I stayed I would be instantly telegraphing my insecurity about leaving Melissa in the company of two men, and I didn't relish the idea of sitting through another two or three frames of snooker.

"Here's the room key. If you don't come back by midnight, I'm sending out a posse."

I tried to sound as unconcerned as possible, but inwardly I was distraught that she was remaining in the bar with two strangers. As I readied for bed, I decided to leave the door unlocked on the offhand chance that she might misplace the key.

I awakened about three hours later and looked at my watch. 1:30 A.M. The bathroom light was on, and I remembered that the room had been completely dark when I had drifted off to sleep. I got up and went into the bathroom and noticed that Melissa's make-up bag was sitting on top of the small table fully opened. I couldn't remember if the bag had been there when I came up to the room at 10:30, but the light being on introduced the possibility that Melissa had come back to the room and left again.

Against my better judgment, I got up, hastily dressed, slightly propped the door and headed down to the lobby. The entire downstairs was completely dark except for the light of two floor lamps as I headed down the corridor to the bar. It too was dark and had the look of being closed for several hours. At the front desk was a framed placard explaining to guests who they should call if assistance was needed during the night.

I headed back to the room, wondering how I could find the room number for Marcus Finch. I was quickly concluding that Melissa must be with one (or both) of the two Aussies. My imagination began to invent all sorts of situations, and as I climbed back into bed, sleep seemed only a remote possibility.

I lay there thinking that Melissa might return at any moment, that she had just gone to one of their rooms for a nightcap. It occurred to me that I was essentially in the same situation that Richard Benjamin had been subjected to less than a week ago. Maybe it was divine retribution, and if so, whoever had designed my punishment was being surgically precise. It was almost identical to Richard's situation except that he knew where Teresa was spending the night.

I thought about the night when I had tried to contact Catherine after we had been separated for almost three months. Jenny was staying with me for the weekend, and after she went to bed I sat up and watched Sleeper, the Woody Allen–Diane Keaton film that Catherine and I used to watch together, doubled over with laughter. About one hour into the film, I picked up the phone and called her. It was only 10:30 P.M., and I knew she would still be up on a Saturday night. I let it ring five or six times and then hung up before the answering machine came on.

I should have left it at that, but instead I called her again in thirty minutes. This time, on the message I tried to sound as breezy and unconcerned as possible, but it had already occurred to me that she was probably out with Brian, who Jenny had mentioned at dinner was "Mom's new friend."

Even though Catherine and I had agreed that it would be fine for each of us to date other people during the separation, the idea had remained only a theory for me, and so for the first time I was confronted with the reality of her being with another man. As it turned out, between 11:00 P.M. and 4:00 A.M., I left eight or nine messages on her phone, each one more pathetic than the previous one, so that later the next day, when I returned Jenny to what had been our family home, Catherine simply said that she had listened to the first three messages and erased the rest. I said that I was sorry, but from that point on she began to protect her personal space in ways that were completely foreign to the bonds we once had in our marriage. Because of my impetuous suspicions, I ripped away whole sections of the fabric of friendship that we were both committed to when we agreed to separate.

As I lay there watching the bedside clock click down the minutes to 2:00 A.M., I thought about how I should react to Melissa's return, even if it didn't occur until dawn. Through earlier painful situations like the one with Catherine, I had learned that being confrontational or acting wounded would be the impetus for the relationship to begin a slow dissolve. Most women want their freedom, and once they detect barriers they begin to move away—consciously or subconsciously—to an equilibrium where they are fully accepted for who they are and who they desire to be.

I heard the door lock quietly unlatch. Melissa was making every effort to be quiet, and when she slipped into the bathroom and turned on the light, I lay there undecided as to whether I should feign sleep or pretend to have just awakened. Several minutes later she turned out the bathroom light and quietly slipped into bed. As she snuggled closer to me I realized that although she was completely naked, she was warm.

"Warm," I thought, "from another man's bed."

"James, are you awake?"

"I'm partly awake; is everything OK?"

"I need for you to hold me close to you."

As she said this, she placed her right leg over mine so that she was almost lying on top of me.

"I want you to hold me. I'm feeling a little frightened."

Was she frightened by what had just happened with the Aussies? A part of me wanted a fuller explanation, but thinking better of it, I pulled her closer to me, allowing her to know that she was now safe. My heart began to pound as she moved her head from my shoulder to the center of my chest. I leaned over and kissed her hair and with that her lips kissed my neck and then my lips. Whatever else I was feeling at that moment quickly evaporated. I was hopelessly infatuated with her, and I no longer cared about her motives, her veracity, or even what may have happened with Marcus Finch and John Langford. Melissa and I were alone together in sub-Saharan Africa, and for the moment, nothing else could possibly matter.

CHAPTER EIGHT

CHARLIE WAS AWAKENED AROUND 2:00 A.M. BY THE sound of a truck coming up the driveway. He turned on the bedside lamp and went to the window. It was dark in the driveway, but even in the darkness he could see that it was the mechanic's truck.

The truck idled for a moment and then a man got out and began walking towards the woodpile. Charlie pulled on his shirt and pants and rushed downstairs. As he pulled open the front door, the man ran back to the cab and struggled for a moment to get it into reverse. As the gears grinded, Charlie began walking towards the cab.

"Where's Jenny?" he shouted, but the man's head was already turned away from him as the truck kicked into reverse and backed down the drive. Charlie had enough presence to glance at the license plate but in the glare of the headlights all he was able to see were the letters WL followed by three or four numbers. It was clearly an Alberta plate. As the truck faded into the darkness, Charlie stood in the drive and shivered from the shock of the cold and the realization that his worst fears about Jenny could not now be disputed. He wondered where the man had left her and whether she was dead or alive. Knowing that he couldn't go back to sleep, Charlie sat down next to the fire, which was now just a few glowing embers.

"He came back for something," Charlie thought, "But what could have possibly been the significance of the woodpile?"

Even though it was the middle of the night, Charlie found a flashlight in the kitchen drawer, put on his coat, gloves, and boots, and went out to investigate. The woodpile was partially covered with several inches of snow from the previous afternoon, and Charlie began to methodically brush away the layers, not knowing what he was looking for. After about thirty minutes of carefully removing snow and looking around the woodshed, his fingers were beginning to numb in the subzero temperatures. He decided to resume searching in the morning, and knowing that he would need wood for the morning fire, he lifted two logs from the top of the pile. As he did so, he noticed a white object fall off to the side. Jenny's phone! Charlie dropped the logs and headed back into the house clutching the phone and staring at the face of it, somehow thinking that she might have left a last-second text as she was forced against her will into the truck.

Undoubtedly, the mechanic had grabbed it out of her hand and flung it to the back of the woodpile as he manhandled her into the passenger side of the truck. Knowing that his phone number could be in the phone's call history, he had come back to retrieve the phone and destroy the one piece of evidence that would link him to Jenny's abduction. Charlie theorized all of this on his brief walk back into the house, and now he sat down next to the fire, still clutching the ice-cold phone in his right hand.

The entire face of the phone was completely fogged over, and Charlie noticed that ice crystals had formed beneath the screen. He instinctively placed the phone in his armpit, desperately thinking that once the phone returned to room temperature it would revive itself. After about thirty minutes, the phone was warmed up enough for Charlie to try turning the phone on. It was unresponsive. He removed the back of the phone and took out the battery. He noticed that the battery and the inside encasement were damp, and he took Jenny's hair dryer to attempt to dry out the interior.

He could imagine some techie telling him later that, "You should never use a hair dryer to attempt to dry out a cell phone," but with each step in the process, he was hoping to see the screen suddenly light up. After about an hour of failed attempts, he placed the disassembled phone on the kitchen counter and headed back up to bed. There was already a growing fear in his heart that he was in way over his head, that his support system was crumbling around him. His marriage, his job, and his relationship with his real father were all now in jeopardy, and time was working against him in every imaginable way.

If this had happened just six months earlier, he would have called his mother. She would know people in Canada who could bring back a semblance of normalcy and could begin a process of sorting things out. She had interceded for him on countless other occasions by her sheer force of character, by her remarkable demeanor that persuaded all sorts of people to come to her aid, even if she had only known them for ten minutes. Since her death, Charlie had attempted to transfer some of that dependence to Heather, but Heather often had her own agenda, and recently she lacked the initiative in social situations to navigate her way as successfully as Teresa. Heather now was not an ally, but rather another obstacle in the entanglement that was becoming his tragic reality.

As he drifted off to sleep, he imagined himself breaking the windshield of the truck with a crowbar, shattering the glass as the man attempted to put the truck in reverse. He imagined himself overpowering the man and throwing the keys to the truck into the woodshed. He saw himself standing over the man with the raised crowbar and demanding that he tell him what he had done with

Jenny. In his exhausted state he imagined the Royal Canadian Mounted Police arriving and congratulating him for apprehending one of the most heinous sex offenders in the province of Alberta. In short, he imagined himself to be self-sufficient and heroic, two qualities that he often admired in others, but as yet had remained only a fiction of his adult life.

CHAPTER NINE

THE MEIKLES HOTEL IN HARARE IS REGARDED BY MOST as the epicenter of social, political, and governmental interaction in the capital. Like the Bulawayo Club and The Victoria Falls Hotel, the Meikles Hotel serves as a reminder of Zimbabwe's colonial history as well as its forward-looking intentions as an independent African nation, and the clientele reflect both the legacy of Southern Rhodesia and the vibrancy of a newly formed Zimbabwe.

Our arrival at Meikles after an overnight train from Bulawayo was fairly uneventful, save for the early morning entrance of the porter in our double berth just as Melissa was standing completely naked at the sink. I was amazed at his composure as he asked without a blink whether we wanted coffee or tea to begin our day.

As we stood at reception, I contemplated whether we should again register as Mr. and Mrs. Monroe or as separate parties. I knew that the bill for our accommodations would eventually be submitted to AFREA in Nairobi, and I wondered how scrupulous the bursar would be about the charges. By this point Melissa and I were more than just travel companions, and I didn't want to put her in an awkward position with the front desk. In the end we registered as husband and wife, although I knew that I would introduce her at the reception as Miss Melissa Samuel.

That afternoon I contacted my friend, Mr. Koffi Saungweme, Senior Program Officer for the African Capacity Building Foundation, and I invited him to join Melissa and me for a drink at Meikles before the reception. Like most Zimbabweans, he was extremely friendly and helpful, and I knew that he could bring me up to speed on hot topics that others would be chatting about at the reception.

Melissa decided to wear her dress from Maxine's for the meeting with Koffi, since the reception would begin after our drink, and she took my breath away when she appeared from the bathroom at a few minutes before 4:00. As we emerged from the lobby elevator, Koffi was sitting in one of Meikles' large wingback chairs, and he gave me one of his broad smiles.

"James, it is fabulous to see you again."

"You as well, Koffi. I want you to meet my friend, Melissa Samuel."

Whatever surprise Koffi may have been registering at my attending the reception with a woman was eclipsed by his equally instant infatuation with Melissa.

"Haven't we met before, Miss Samuel?"

Koffi had been single for as long as I had known him, and he had learned some of the basics of how to talk to women. Melissa had already primed herself to be miss congeniality with all the prospective employers that afternoon, so I simply sat back and observed the two of them in action.

"I don't think we've met, unless you've been to Australia."

I thought of my own flirtatious conversation with Melissa before her rescue at the Devil's Pool. She was very adept at this kind of playful banter.

"I've been to Perth, but that was on a container ship when I was much younger."

"Perth is a continent away from Melbourne and Sydney, but at least you can say that you've been Down Under—which is less than James can say."

Normally I would have said something in response, but I simply smiled, hoping that Koffi would be content with a brief introduction to Melissa and leave it at that.

"How are things at ACBF?"

I knew my inquiry would also play to his conversational strengths, and as I had hoped, he took the bait.

"Capacity building in Africa is such a slow process!"

I could tell that he was giving us a preamble to a twenty-minute explanation in which he would attempt to impress Melissa with his knowledge of capacity building in sub-Saharan Africa, including all of the outreach programs that he had helped to initiate.

I took the opportunity to wander over to the registration desk, where I hoped to see the guest list of those invited to the reception. Standing next to the desk was David Fortran, a fellow WB employee who I had not seen in over a year. David and I trained together at AFREA in Nairobi, and while I had been assigned to Zimbabwe and Mozambique, David had remained in Kenya, content to work on WB projects that focused on improving infrastructure in the Rift Valley and on the coast near Mombasa.

He had a reputation at AFREA as a womanizer, and during the six months that we trained together, he kept a running count of his weekend conquests that included women from every continent with the possible exception of Antarctica. Despite his exploits with women, he was a very effective analyst, and he was often called upon to sort out some donor-related juggernaut where Bank interests were being compromised by overreaching government regulations. He was also somewhat humble about his work-related accomplishments, since we both had learned early on that the culture of the Bank required an understated efficiency that was often disarming in our work with international clients. Frequently a negotiation would turn upon our ability not to reveal the Bank's potential involvement in a project, and thus pressure the other side to make a greater financial commitment.

"How are you, David? You must have twisted their arms for them to allow you to leave Nairobi."

He wheeled around and I could tell that he was struggling to put my face to a name. In true diplomatic style, he retrieved my last name at the last possible second.

"Mr. Monroe! The Bank actually sent me down here to check up on you. Now that I've seen you, I can return to Nairobi." We shook hands, and in that split second he remembered my name and used it to exonerate himself of any temporary lapse in memory. "How are you, James?"

"Never been better, and I'm actually headed up your way next week to have lunch with a former Indian official from Maharashtra."

"That road project has been in the planning stages for at least five years. If they don't get off the dime, we are going to pull the funding. Problem is the bidding process in Bombay. It has been out for bid three or four times and the government always finds a reason to start over. The corruption is overwhelming."

"David, I want you to meet a friend of mine, but you have to promise to leave her alone."

"I only make promises when it involves Bank business. Otherwise all bets are off."

We began to walk towards Koffi and Melissa, and I noticed that they had been joined by Ibrahim Saungweme, the editor of The Economist, a very timely and informative journal whose many contributions included both government and private sector people of influence—the core constituency of Zimbabwean commerce.

"Melissa, I want you to meet my colleague, David Fortran. We trained together in AFREA in Nairobi."

Melissa, already surrounded by two men, was pleased to add two more. I was surprised when she stole Koffi's earlier question as it seemed repetitive and out of place, especially with Koffi still seated next to her.

"Mr. Fortran, I feel like we've met before?"

David was quick on the uptake. "You just stole my line."

"And mine." Koffi was mumbling under his breath and winked at Melissa.

Before Melissa had a chance to respond, I quickly changed the subject to our drink order, and I motioned over one of the waiters who was circulating through the lobby. I now recognized why Melissa thought she had met David. He and the man who rescued her at the Devil's Pool could have been brothers. It was their similar physique, but more than that, it was their facial bone structure. I thought of how Melissa and the man at the Devil's Pool were locked together in their common desire to survive, and I began to imagine how firmly those moments had been imprinted on her subconscious.

When our drinks arrived, we all headed into the hotel ballroom, and I was chagrined to see Melissa slip her arm through David's elbow as we progressed into the reception. It was only a friendly gesture, but I had imagined her next to me at this moment countless times since our departure from Victoria Falls. In any event, Melissa wasted no time in her quest to circulate through the entire room, and she used David, Koffi, and me as her anchors to produce the multiple introductions she needed to find "the" contact who might mention a job opening.

As I predicted, Pierre Jonquin was in the room, and when I introduced him to Melissa, they both started chatting in fluent French. Several other Francophone countries were represented as well, and now Melissa was in an animated discussion with four French diplomats.

She was remarkably at ease with people she was only meeting for the first time, and I noticed that she had the endearing habit of lightly touching the arm of the person she was addressing, a tactic that focused his full attention on her and added a slight flirtation to the moment. Her statuesque demeanor, her perfectly tailored black dress, and the effervescent glow of her lovely face and hair reminded me of the image of her floating goddess-like above the lip of the Falls. Melissa was able to draw energy and confidence from any milieu that provided a challenge—whether the inexorable current at the Devil's Pool or finding a job in a room full of diplomats.

I admired her because I had seen both sides of her—ice in her veins in some situations and incredible warmth and affection in others. I envied her innate spirituality and her intellectual interest in philosophy. Even as I watched her conversing in fluent French, I imagined her equating something just said with her knowledge of Camus. There was a universality about her that allowed her to reflect a goddess-like power combined with an intense personal desire to live every moment to its fullest degree. Beyond her physical beauty, it was this capacity for intensity that set her apart. She was able to draw upon that flaming sword when the situation called for it, and as I watched her shoulders pull back and relax, I knew that one of the French diplomats had just offered her a job.

Back in our room that evening, Melissa's joy at the job offer was tempered by her mention of a simultaneous request for a reference from the French embassy in Sydney. Even though she would be working for the French consulate in Nairobi, she thought there was a reasonable chance that someone in Nairobi would know a former colleague in Sydney.

"How can I sidestep the reference request? I should never have mentioned Sydney in the first place."

As she said this, she moved closer to me and I helped her unzip her dress. I felt like we were a married couple discussing the pros and cons of an evening out as we readied for bed.

"If they call the ambassador, there's a chance he will ruin my chances."

"Why would he do that?"

Melissa was now standing in just her black underwear in front of the full-length mirror, and she was brushing out her hair. I pretended to be busy composing a Telex to Nairobi, but even though I had seen her naked before, she looked even more provocative this evening.

"I had this very awkward weekend traveling with the ambassador to Auckland. It happened about six months before I left the embassy."

Melissa paused from her hair brushing and looked directly at me as if to emphasize the point.

"He assumed way too much. When we arrived at the hotel in Auckland, he had only booked one room. When I insisted on having my own room, he pouted and barely spoke to me that weekend or when we returned."

I thought of how I didn't disturb Melissa when she had fallen asleep fully clothed in my room at The Victoria Falls Hotel, and how careful I had been the first night on the train to be content with her sleeping by my side. Until this moment I had no idea how prescient that strategy had been, and now I began to second guess my initial assumptions about where she had been late at night at the Bulawayo Club. Yes, she was undoubtedly flirtatious with men, but that flirtatiousness might only rarely transition into promiscuity. If that was the case, the week we had spent together became even more significant. She was allowing me into her world, the same world that she had barred from other interested men.

"Who from the French consulate offered you a job?"

"His name is Gerard Hugel. He gave me his card."

As it turned out, I had worked with Gerard Hugel on a Bank project in Tanzania. The French were one of the three or four Western donors, and Gerard was representing their interests from the French embassy in Cairo.

"I know Gerard. We worked together in Tanzania. If you want, I will talk to him about your suitability. He certainly can't question your knowledge of French."

As she had done several times previously, she crossed the room and kissed me.

"Can you talk to him in the morning?"

"Let's find out if he's staying here."

I dialed the front desk and asked to be connected to M. Hugel. As soon as the call was put through, I hung up the phone.

"He's here. I'll intercept him at breakfast in the morning. I'll mention to him that he should snap you up before you take another offer."

"I did actually get another offer."

"Let me guess, David Fortran offered you a job."

"He's looking for an administrative assistant at AFREA in Nairobi."

"Of course he is. He wrote the job description as you two walked into the reception together. What did you tell him?"

"I told him that I would be in Nairobi by Tuesday and that we could talk more then."

"I thought you were meeting Kate and Trevor in South Africa next week?"

"That doesn't make much sense if I have a job offer in Nairobi."

"Does that mean we are traveling together to Nairobi?"

"Only if you don't mind your new best friend tagging along?"

Melissa turned off the two floor lamps and the bathroom light and sat next to me on the bed. Her long curls fell across her neck and shoulders and cascaded over her breasts. She placed her left hand lightly on my side and leaned over to whisper in my ear.

"Whenever this stops feeling right for either of us, we need to agree that we will end it without further expectations."

It was an odd and unexpected comment from her, and a proviso that I had failed to follow when I intuitively knew that earlier relationships had run their course. I began to respond, but as I did, she placed two fingers across my lips and then carefully removed my shirt. My imagination was racing in anticipation of what might come next. But instead of crawling into bed next to me, she allowed her head to rest on my chest, her left ear over my heart, her right hand gently massaging my hair.

We stayed like this for several minutes and I began to sense that Melissa wanted our intimacy that evening to be something beyond just the physical, that she wanted the two of us to experience a spiritual oneness that had been the source of my initial attraction to her our first day together at Victoria Falls.

As if to verify my intuition, Melissa now sat next to me, her back perfectly straight, her feet and ankles tucked neatly under her in a meditative pose. She began to lightly touch my face, shoulders, and neck, allowing one finger to trace behind another until this transitioned into a quick successive touch of fingertips that felt like showers of raindrops.

As she became more creative with these light fingertip touches I began to hear the same melodious Hebrew or Arabic phrases from our first night that were initially a whisper and then a faint song. At one point she paused, placing both of her hands first around my feet and then in my hair, and as she was moving away from my head, she whispered into my ear.

"You are greatly loved, James. Yahweh wants you to know that you are greatly loved."

At that she put her face next to mine and held it there for several minutes. What happened next was our transition into transcendence. As she pulled her legs back into a lotus position, her knees were now touching my side and her arms were extended so that her hands were just inches away from my skin.

She began to breathe in a more rhythmical pattern, and now her long exhales were punctuated by short gasps that sounded like small ecstatic whimpers. As she began to move her hands in that several-inch space just above my legs and chest, I could feel the heat from her hands begin to increase.

It was a heat that I had never experienced before. There was both a warmth and an exhilaration that messaged both intense love and sensual stimulation. Melissa brought me to a place that was way beyond the physical. I began to sense that I was floating, that my body was still firmly on the bed, but my spirit was soaring to a place that only the two of us could fully comprehend.

She shifted to her knees and using her long, curly hair she began to bathe my entire body so that only her curls were touching my skin. The effect of her luxurious hair moving back and forth, up and down my body was incredibly erotic. She moaned a little as we both experienced the sweetness of that sacred space, and I could only think of the fragility of what had just occurred. Despite the beauty of our intimacy and her seeming ability to give herself completely to another person, I fell asleep with the reminder that she had prefaced our lovemaking by reminding me that she might leave at any time.

CHAPTER TEN

Charlie awakened to the sound of sleet tapping against the window. He looked at the clock—9:30 A.M. He had finally fallen asleep around 5:00 and now the events of the night before came rushing back.

Jenny was gone; the man in the truck had returned in the middle of the night; Jenny's phone was inoperable; and since it was Saturday, James Monroe was scheduled to arrive home. In Heather's mind he was only a few hours away from Winnetka and would be home in plenty of time to take Ryan to the all-day indoor soccer tournament.

He wandered downstairs and made coffee, trying to prioritize who he should call first. He knew he should call Heather, but the prospect of beginning his day with her prosecutorial reaction made him want to connect with his father first. At least if he talked to James, he could honestly say to Heather that his father had asked him to stay.

He was about to dial Vancouver information when he noticed that he had missed three earlier calls from Heather. Looking at the call history, he realized that it was 11:45 A.M. in Winnetka, just about the time when he could not possibly get back to Winnetka in time, even if he drove straight through. He clicked on the most recent call and hit dial. He couldn't imagine what he would say to Heather, since now she would have to find someone to take Ryan to soccer.

"Why don't you answer your phone?" It was Heather's typical salutation—starting the conversation midstream.

"I must have put the ringer on mute."

"Please tell me you are almost home."

"I'm actually still in Lake Louise."

Charlie knew that this information would bring silence on the other end, and he also knew that Heather's tone—still fairly neutral—was about to change completely. He braced himself for the onslaught.

"What the hell, Charlie! Why did you lie to me?"

"How did I lie?"

He knew that she was referring to his earlier promise to be home by Sunday, but he couldn't think of any other response.

"You told me you were heading home two days ago. Do Ryan and I mean nothing to you?"

He knew that she was closing in for the kill, but he was suddenly out of excuses.

"Of course, I care about you and Ryan."

"You know what? Just stay out in fucking Canada. If you cared about us, you'd be honest with me, and you'd be almost home by now."

Charlie was out of responses, and he allowed the silence to sear into the phone.

"What am I supposed to tell Ryan? Really Charlie, what kind of father are you?" Heather knew that the bad father accusation would be the one that would sting the most, and she kept going. "Who am I going to find in the middle of a weekend to take him to soccer? I have to be at that meeting by 12:15. Unlike you, I keep my commitments. As usual, Charlie, it's all about you. Do you ever think about your family and their needs?"

Charlie thought about telling Heather about the late night visit, the phone, and how he had only had four hours of sleep. But Heather had already voiced her incredulity that Jenny had been kidnapped, and because of his earlier dishonesty, he had essentially lost all credibility with his wife.

"I'm going to come home as soon as I can."

Heather allowed the weakness of his response to linger for a moment before her closing volley of criticism.

"You know what, Charlie. I have put up with your insecurities and your dishonesty for over ten years. I'm tired of being a single parent who gets zero support from her spouse. The crazy thing is that I am constantly defending you, even lying for you when your partners call here because you won't answer your phone. I give and I give, and I get nothing in return. Other people might like you, but as a husband and a father you are a complete disappointment. Other husbands keep their word. Other fathers spend time with their kids, so really, don't come home. Don't come home until you are ready to grow up and act like a man."

Heather knew that this final jab at his manhood would sink the knife of bitterness deep into his gut, and in her usual style, she decided to end the phone call before he was able to respond. "Goodbye, Charlie. If you ever decide that you are willing to give something to this marriage, give me a call. Otherwise it's probably better if we don't communicate for a while. I'm tired of pretending to have a happy marriage when it is really a disaster."

Charlie saw his screen go blank as Heather ended the call. He sat at the kitchen table and looked outside at the sleet that had now turned to snow. He thought about all of the selfish things Heather had done since they had been married, and how he had adopted a passive-aggressive response that allowed him to agree with her in the short term while subtly undermining her and their marriage over the long haul. There was a part of him that wanted it to come to this. She had suggested a period of no communication, a trial separation, and perhaps this was the opening he had longed for. What would it be like to be divorced? He knew that Jenny had spoken about their father's divorce, and at the thought of his father he dialed information for Vancouver and asked to be connected to the Stanley Park precinct of the Vancouver police.

"Stanley Park."

"Yes, where would my brother be able to stay for a night or two until I am able to come get him? He is out of money and he needs a place to stay."

"We send all of the short termers to Victoria House. They will feed and house him for up to a week."

"Do you possibly have their phone number?"

"Just a minute."

While he was away from the phone Charlie thought about also asking him for the acceptable timeframe for reporting missing persons, but reconsidered after calibrating the potential suspicion that might be raised by such an odd request.

"604-927-1853."

"Thanks very much."

Charlie carefully dialed the number, realizing that his real father might answer the phone.

"Victoria House."

"Is James Monroe there?"

"Left yesterday for Lake Louise. Can I help with something?"

"This is his son calling."

"James has never mentioned a son to me, and I've known him for over twenty years."

"Am I talking to Rob?"

"Yep, I'm Rob Curtin. The two of us run this place."

"Rob, if James left there yesterday, how long does it take him to get to Lake Louise?"

"Can you tell me again how you are related to James?"

"Actually Jenny and I are related, and I've never met James."

"It's an eight- or nine-hour trip; usually he stays over in Kamloops. He left here at 4:00

P.M. yesterday, so he should be there before noon today—unless the weather is bad."

"Thanks so much, Rob."

"Tell me your name again."

"Charlie Benjamin."

Charlie now realized that James might arrive in the next two hours, and he thought about how he would break the news about Jenny. He also realized that this might be the last opportunity he would have to wash away his fingerprints from around the bathtub. It seemed unlikely that police detectives would ever be in the house looking for fingerprints, but he had already decided that he would not include the bathtub interlude in any narrative that he would give about his twenty-four hours with Jenny.

As he entered the bathroom and knelt down by the tub, he noticed the bottle of shampoo that he had groped for under the tub. He instinctively took the bottle and placed it in the very back of the small bathroom closet. The entire room smelled like Jenny's fresh bath, and the snow had already covered the skylight so that the bathroom was dark despite the late morning hour.

As Charlie took a small cloth and began to wash down the sides of the tub, he remembered reading about Jewish purification rituals where the entire body—including the hair—was washed in preparation for burial. If Jenny was in fact dead, he would tell James about his brief time with her as she bathed—sister and brother finally united during a purification ritual preparing her for burial. It was a morbid thought, but he forced himself to consider it.

As he started to wipe away possible fingerprints from the floor surrounding the tub, he heard several long honks in the driveway. He ran to the bedroom window and in the light snowfall he saw his father emerge from the cab of a late-model pickup. He looked older than the pictures of him in the living room, and his gray hair was cut very short. Even from the window, Charlie could see that

James was thin and fit—a man who had continued to be active into his sixties. He had on jeans and a brown leather jacket, and Charlie noticed a cowboy hat on the dashboard of the truck.

His heart was full of anticipation as he bounded down the stairs and opened the front door. As soon as James saw Charlie, his face broadened into a welcoming smile.

"Are you Teresa Benjamin's son? Are you Charlie Benjamin?"

"I am. I think you knew my mom in Africa."

"Your mom was quite a woman. Someone who I will always cherish and remember."

"She thought a lot of you as well. In fact, she mentioned your name on her deathbed."

Both men just stood there allowing the import of Teresa's death to be the initial nexus of their reunion. They had both known and loved Teresa, and their reunion must have been something she had dreamed about for decades. Now that they were meeting for the first time, they both found it difficult to express their latent emotion and their common expectation.Charlie knew that he should immediately tell James about Jenny's disappearance, but he wanted the positive aspects of their first father-son meeting to linger for a minute more. Instead of mentioning Jenny, he returned to Teresa.

"She died just five months ago—late October."

James knew that he would have the opportunity to talk more about Teresa, and so he decided to transition back to the moment. His mantra since moving to Canada was to live in the present.

"In any event, Charlie, welcome to Lake Louise. I assume Jenny has taken good care of you."

"She took very good care of me, but she's been missing since yesterday afternoon."

James stopped in his tracks and looked into Charlie's eyes.

"Where is she? What do you mean 'missing'?"

"We were cross-country skiing yesterday afternoon on the

Lake Moraine trail. She came back here to get her phone. She didn't want to miss your call. When I came back she was gone."

"There's got to be more to it than that."

"A mechanic was here yesterday morning. He came back in his truck last night. When I approached him he sped off. I got part of his license plate."

James's eyes were still fixed on Charlie. Charlie thought about all of the prevarication that his father had to deal with in Vancouver. All of those made-up stories that he undoubtedly had heard from people hoping to stay for an extra week at the shelter. He suddenly realized that James had every right to be skeptical.

"Did you check the trail?"

"I didn't check the trail because Jenny's cross-country skis were propped up next to the door when I got back. Besides, I found her hair clip on the floor of the car, and why would the mechanic return in the middle of the night? He must have been looking for her phone that I later found in the woodpile."

Charlie realized that his explanation sounded rushed and disjointed. There were too many disparate parts to his explanation. It was beginning to sound like a hastily thrown-together alibi, and as the two of them continued to stand in the doorway, Charlie wanted to reassure his father in some way. Both of them realized that Jenny's disappearance now presented a barrier to what had begun as a happy reunion of father and son.

"We need to check the trail. For all you know she injured herself as she was skiing back to find you. Jenny has several other pairs of skis; she may have used one of those."

As James slipped by him and into the front hallway, Charlie felt foolish and bewildered. He noticed that his father was leaving on his coat.

"Of course I should have checked the trail," Charlie thought. "I should have checked it as soon as I found Jenny missing."

"So you heard a truck last night in the driveway?"

"It was the mechanic's truck; I even saw him get out and look around."

When Charlie started to explain about finding the phone, he brought the disassembled phone to the kitchen table like a child might bring a broken toy to his father. James looked at it, reassembled it, and for a moment the screen lit up as if it were coming on. After a flicker it went dark again. Charlie regarded the flicker as the first hopeful sign since her disappearance, and for a moment he thought that Jenny was now somehow aware that her father was home.

Charlie didn't mention being in the bathroom while Jenny was about to wash her hair or the potential fingerprint issue, but he was relieved to tell someone other than Heather what had happened during the past twenty-four hours. As he finished the entire narrative, James began to buckle on the cross-country ski boots that Charlie had worn the day before.

"I'm going to ski the trail. Why don't you fix us some lunch and I will be back in about ninety minutes."

Charlie watched as his father strapped on the cross-country skis and headed for the trail. As he fixed some soup and sandwiches, he hoped that his father did not find Jenny on the five-mile loop. If he did find her, it meant she had been injured and had spent the night on the trail in ten-degree weather. Whatever her condition at this point, Charlie would be seen as being negligent and culpable if she had debilitating injuries, or worse, if she had died. But her being on the trail would not explain the mechanic's night visit to the woodpile or Jenny's hair clip in the front seat of the car. And if she had returned for her phone, why would she have left it on the woodpile?

True to his word, Charlie's father skied back into the driveway ninety minutes after his departure. Watching him remove his skis, Charlie already knew from his unhurried demeanor that he had not found Jenny.

"We've done our due diligence. She's not on the trail and it hasn't snowed enough to completely cover a body. She wouldn't have skied off the trail, so now we are most likely looking for another explanation."

As the two of them sat down for a late lunch, Charlie felt as if he had gained some credibility. Now the late night truck and the frozen phone seemed to be more important factors in Jenny's disappearance. Whatever blame James had been assigning to Charlie was now replaced with a desire for more information about the events leading to Jenny's disappearance.

"Remind me again how you knew I was in Lake Louise?"

There was a long pause, and both men looked over at the crackling fire before Charlie responded.

"My mother told me on her deathbed that you are my real father. That she met you in Africa. I found your address in her wallet after she died."

There was a brief pause as they both returned to the awkwardness they had experienced when James first arrived.

"I knew that you had been born, but it wasn't my place to tell Teresa how to handle things. I had already complicated her life. It was probably better all around that only the two of us knew the truth. But I'm glad that you drove all the way out here to see me. Most men who have never had a son secretly wish for one, as I always have. Did you tell Jenny?"

"I told her on Thursday night. She didn't take it well at first, but she was better on Friday morning when we decided to go skiing."

"Tell me what she said."

Charlie thought for a second, trying to remember Jenny's actual words.

"Not then, but earlier, when I first arrived, she said that the two of you were very close—that she is the most important person in your life, that the two of you are as close as a father and daughter can possibly be."

Charlie looked across the table and noticed that James was gazing across the room at the picture of Jenny and him outside a cave. She could only have been twelve or thirteen. Charlie could sense that James was on the verge of losing the equilibrium that he had carefully kept intact since his arrival, and he decided to quickly change the subject.

"Who is that woman standing next to you at the top of the falls?"

James shifted his gaze off to the right, as if he was looking at the falls photograph for the first time.

"That's Melissa Samuel, an Australian woman who I also knew in Africa. Quite a woman, but she couldn't hold a candle to your mother."

"Someday I would love to hear how you and mom met. It must have been quite an adventure."

"Probably a story for another time. Right now we need to focus on finding Jenny."

Charlie was relieved to realize that Jenny's disappearance was now not completely his responsibility—that moment by moment he was gaining credibility with James, that together the two of them would decide the next course of action. His father's calm, organized demeanor was already influencing Charlie, and he wondered what he would now be like if James had been in his life all along as he matured into adulthood.

"Shouldn't we call the police?"

Charlie realized that the knee-jerk reactions that he had been experiencing since yesterday would now be tempered by his father's organized plan for how to proceed.

"We probably should wait until late afternoon to call the RCMP. Then we can honestly say it's been twenty-four hours. What we can do is find out what the neighbors may have seen. Despite its large geography, this part of Alberta is like a small town. I'm going to take a drive down to the village to talk to my buddies at the convenience. Do you remember the color of the truck? Was there lettering on the side?"

"I can't be sure about any lettering, but the truck was gray or maybe moss green."

"Alberta plates?"

"I'm sure about the Alberta plates, and the first two letters were WL."

"Was the truck bed a lift?"

"Pretty sure it had double tires on the back with a big flatbed—not sure about the lift."

"That's a start. Someone in the village will know the truck."

"I remember Jenny saying that she had called a mechanic in Banff."

"If he's from Banff that makes it more difficult, but I also know people down there. I'm taking a drive. Anything else you remember?"

"The guy was probably 5'10"—kind of heavyset, with a beard."

"Most men in Alberta have a beard, so that probably doesn't help. Why don't you get some rest and I'll be back in an hour or so."

As Charlie climbed the stairs he felt the same security he had felt as a child when his parents had put him to bed in the early evening and he had drifted off reassured by the sound of their voices from the living room below. Somehow with his father there, Charlie no longer felt overwhelmed and afraid. "It's good to be home," he repeated to himself, and with that he allowed his body to relax for the first time since Jenny's disappearance.

CHAPTER ELEVEN

THE THREE-HOUR KENYA AIRWAYS FLIGHT FROM HARARE to Nairobi occurs three times a day and prices vary according to the time of day and the time of year. I had originally been booked on a late Monday afternoon flight, which was to land in Nairobi shortly after dinner. Since I had reservations at The Norfolk Hotel, which is a little out of town, my plan was to first get a cab to The Carnivore (my favorite Nairobi restaurant and the only place in the city where you will find both ostrich and crocodile on the menu), and then go to the hotel.

But once Melissa decided to join me, we rebooked on a late morning flight, which would allow us to meet Gerard Hugel for a drink at 5:00 P.M. on the Delamere Terrace of The Norfolk. I was personally paying for her ticket, and I also ended up paying the ticket change fee for my original booking, since I thought it unfair to charge the Bank for a change that only reflected my preference to fly with Melissa to Nairobi.

It was the first time I had been on a plane with a woman since the Flight of Angels with Teresa, and as we taxied down the runway, I thought of all that had happened in just one week. With Teresa, the boundaries of our relationship were immovable. Yes, we had slept together, but she was on holiday in Africa with her husband and her children. I couldn't imagine any scenario that would cause the two of us to ever leave together for another country.

Yet in comparing Teresa to Melissa, I was aware of the magnanimity in Teresa that was especially there when we said farewell at the train station. Melissa was undoubtedly the most fascinating woman I had ever known. She was beautiful, athletic, and consummately graceful. She was well read, philosophical, and mysteriously spiritual. She actually glowed with a degree of intensity that made her charismatic—especially around men. But despite all of that, I was beginning to fear that there was a part of her that I would never know, that would always be held in reserve. Her comment of a few nights ago—that both of us should feel free to leave if our feelings ever changed—reminded me that Melissa favored contingency over stability. She valued the easy exit, and if needed, the closing of the door. Better to leave the messy situations of life behind when the future held such an effervescent dawn. She had essentially ditched Kate and Trevor, leaving her possible reunion with them completely up in the air. Already I was fearful that either Gerard Hugel or David Fortran would win her away from me once we got to Nairobi. But as I sat next to her and felt the plane climb effortlessly into the sub-Saharan sky, I was powerless to change course. I knew that I would pursue her until every avenue of attraction on my part had been exhausted.

The Norfolk Hotel, like The Victoria Falls Hotel, was built in the early 1900s, and it quickly established itself as the premier watering hole for the rich and famous who visited Kenya. Teddy Roosevelt stayed there when Nairobi was little more than a train stop between Mombasa and Lake Victoria. Later in the century, Winston Churchill stayed at The Norfolk, as did Lord Delamere, the famous British settler for whom the Delamere Terrace is named.

Melissa and I arrived at the hotel by taxi a little before two, and after a late lunch and a nap, we headed down to the Terrace a little before five, only to find Gerard Hugel already at a table for four overlooking the lawn.

After the initial French salutations and faire la bise—air kisses that both Melissa and Gerard had perfected to a T—we ordered gimlets and made small talk in English about the success of the Meikles reception and our flight from Harare.

Clearly this was a social occasion but also a job interview for Melissa, and she was expertly striking just the right tone of only casual interest in the position. I did, however, notice a small furrow in her brow when our drinks arrived and Gerard mentioned that he had spoken to someone at the French Embassy in Sydney about her suitability for the position in Nairobi.

With ice in her veins and without a hint of anxiety, Melissa slowly exhaled.

"I hope the ambassador was around. Obviously he would be supportive in every way possible."

"I'm glad to hear you say that. The ambassador was at a meeting in New Guinea, but I spoke to an attaché, a Michel Dumond, who was very complimentary."

Melissa's face brightened and her shoulders relaxed. I wondered if she had more than a business friendship with Michel, since I could sense her renewed confidence. She recalibrated her next sentence as she delivered it.

"The ambassador and Michel and I worked on many projects together. Next to the ambassador, Michel is the best person you could have spoken to as a reference."

"Your best reference is actually sitting next to you. When James saw me after breakfast the other morning, he couldn't stop singing your praises."

Melissa's knee touched mine under the table and she lightly touched the rim of her glass with her forefinger.

"James has been very generous in introducing me to many of his friends, including you, Gerard. I'm very grateful that you might consider me for the position, and I'm going to suggest that while James has his lunch meeting tomorrow, we could meet for lunch to talk about more of the specifics."

At that Gerard reached across the table and took Melissa's hand. Because of his French heritage, he was completely within the boundaries of social decorum, but like the Aussie he left his hand in hers a few seconds too long and looked a little too intently into her eyes.

"There is a French bistro only a mile from here. James can entertain his guest at the hotel, and I will introduce you to some of my French friends in Nairobi."

I was happy for Melissa that she had finessed the ambassador reference and that she was about to get a job offer from Gerard. But I was fighting my tendency to become insecure and proprietary with her—the same behavior that had produced such disastrous results in the past. At the same time, I feared that I had simply handed her over to him in a brief twenty-minute conversation. Somehow I imagined that Melissa's decision about me—about us—would involve emotional upheaval and angst on both sides. Instead, I imagined them together tomorrow, chatting in French and enjoying lunch, while I met with a disgruntled ex-official from Bombay!

I decided to talk to Melissa that evening after dinner. What I wanted was some statement from her that would indicate feelings that were beyond just gratitude. Even for her to articulate that she valued our friendship would be enough, but somehow we had transitioned from traveling companions to sharing a bed and her emotional equilibrium still registered "status quo."

I knew that to press her on this could be risky. She might simply begin a slow retreat that would leave me feeling alone and ridiculous a month down the road. But to allow her to drift away with either Gerard or David Fortran was equally untenable. Nairobi was an international city, much larger than Harare or Bulawayo, and now I sensed that the inherent boundaries of unfamiliarity were loosening for her. She didn't need me to help her find her way in Nairobi. She had lived alone in Sydney for at least five years, and she had the savvy and sophistication to find what she needed. I was feeling obsolete and foolish that I had not foreseen how Nairobi would change the dynamic between us.

Melissa was sitting on the edge of the bed brushing her hair. We had enjoyed so many evenings like this in the brief time since we met, and the tranquility of the end of the day had become so familiar that we were able to enjoy it together in relative silence. Before I began to speak, I almost reconsidered, remembering her little speech in Harare about exiting if it ever stopped "feeling right." I didn't want to break that magical spell that had begun that first night in Victoria Falls, but in my mind we were at a crossroads.

"Can we talk for a minute about us?"

Melissa stopped the hair brushing for a moment and then resumed. "Sure, what about 'us' do you want to talk about?" She said "us" in a mildly sarcastic tone.

"What I mean is, we have this great relationship, but we never talk about it."

"Talk is what often kills relationships."

"But talk is communication. Isn't it good to communicate?"

"Talking about it makes it a 'thing.' It's better to let it be what it is—something intangible and beyond description." I knew that Melissa read all kinds of Western philosophy, so I was engaging not just her, but every philosopher from Descartes to Sartre. "Don't make me talk about us. Talking about relationships means there's something wrong. Is that what you think?"

"Melissa, if you think our relationship is perfect, then I guess you've answered my question."

"When we listen to music, do we have to analyze it? Can't we just let it be life-giving and leave it at that?"

"I think you're right. I'm sorry I brought it up."

Melissa put down her hairbrush and moved up on the bed so that she was lying with her head on my leg.

"There is something I wanted to talk to you about . . . it concerns your lunch tomorrow with the man from Bombay."

"Have you decided to join us?"

"You know I would have been there if you needed me, but actually I have a small request. It concerns Jonathan."

I had almost forgotten that Melissa's brother was in a Bombay prison, and I instinctively began to touch her arm as a way of reassurance. Her brother's incarceration was the one topic where she had expressed sincere emotion, and I wanted her to be aware of my sympathy.

"How can I help?"

"I don't know who you are meeting with tomorrow, but if he is a former government official, he might know how the legal system works in Bombay. The last time we spoke to Jonathan he talked about needing money for a bribe. Apparently there are a few judges in the system who would accept money to secure his release. The challenge would be finding out who they are and how they might be contacted."

"Of course, I understand."

Melissa's head and her lovely hair now lay across my chest.

As Melissa lay there breathing softly, I knew that Jonathan's incarceration and his possible release were the key to her vulnerability and the place where her heart would be softened. An hour earlier, I had seemingly acquiesced to her desire to remain aloof from the entanglement of relationships; now I could begin to assume the role of knight errant.

I imagined myself calling her from Bombay with news of Jonathan's release—the two of us flying together to Nairobi to be met by Melissa's waiting arms. In my imagination I heard her whisper to me, "In bringing home my brother, you have also won my heart." As I surrendered to a good night's rest, I began to rehearse how I would introduce the topic of Jonathan during my luncheon tomorrow—how I would begin the first step in the long journey to happiness that I had sought for in vain my entire life.

CHAPTER TWELVE

CHARLIE AWAKENED TO THE SOUND OF A TRUCK IN THE driveway, and at first he thought it was *the* truck—returning a second time. But when he went to the window he saw his father getting out of his pickup truck and carrying in a sack of groceries. It was dusk, Charlie guessed five o'clock, and he now knew that he had slept for three hours while James had been away.

"How did you do?" Charlie was still at the top of the stairs and James was now standing just inside the door.

"I did just fine. Come on down and I'll tell you all about it."

As Charlie descended the stairs, he was relieved to feel that someone else was now in charge, and as he helped his father unpack the groceries, he was no longer afraid of the man in the truck or reporting Jenny's disappearance to the RCMP or even of Heather's disquietude. For reasons that Charlie could not quite describe, he felt safe and protected with his father actually there.

"Did you sleep?"

Charlie loved the way that his father put his son's well-being above other concerns.

"Best sleep I've had in months. Any luck in the village?"

James continued to unpack groceries and set aside the chicken and the rice to cook for dinner.

"A Mountie happened to be at the convenience, and I gave him a brief account of Jenny's disappearance. An RCMP detective will be by in the morning to begin an investigation. He said it would be helpful if you wrote down everything that happened—hour by hour."

"Is that all he said?"

"He asked if either of us had actually checked the ski trail."

"We checked the trail. She was abducted."

"They might look at that as only a theory."

"Why would she toss her phone in the woodpile?"

"They could say she put it down in the woodpile while getting logs for the fire."

"Is that what you believe?"

"Of course not. All I'm saying is that they will look at every possibility."

"Then how about the truck in the middle of the night?"

"OK, just to play devil's advocate, they might say that was a midnight dream."

"What?"

"Just to be on the safe side, I would leave out the part you told me about imagining yourself breaking the windshield with a crowbar. That didn't happen, but they might theorize none of it happened—that you imagined all of it."

"So they think she's still out there? Still on the trail?"

"All I'm saying is that they won't assume anything. It's their job to be systematic with any inquiry or investigation. Why don't you work on the report while I fix dinner?"

Charlie acquiesced to his father's calm and principled demeanor. It was as if he were connected to a homing device that kept him always on target, always on point. For as long as Charlie could remember, the man who had raised him, Richard Benjamin, had always been the opposite—subject to situation and circumstance, clever and cunning, but sometimes unreliable. He had a way of negotiating life that was based upon leverage and securing the quick advantage. He placed his own needs before those of others. It was a tenuous way to live, and one that produced a low level of anxiety that was never fully dispelled. The result was a life of pretense where the gambit had to be constantly adjusted to fit the moment, and it was the model that Charlie had been given to follow from a very young age.

It was Teresa who taught him the virtues of kindness and generosity. She was the one who was always ready to forgive and to help others in need. Charlie remembered the Christmas when his college roommate's mother had died unexpectedly the first week of December. Teresa invited him for Christmas and showered him with gifts as if he were part of the family.

She was fiercely independent, and that independence allowed her to live by a different moral code than Richard.It also meant that she rejected Richard's tight hold on life, which ironically kept him from experiencing the vagaries of existence that make life rich and rewarding. If his heart was closed like a tight fist, hers was open and bountifully gracious.

That had been his initial attraction to Heather. When they were dating, and for the first several years of their marriage, she was just like Teresa, open hearted and generous. He liked the way she was able to let go of conflict and find reasons to be happy. But since Ryan was born, she had changed. Now she reminded him more of Richard—keeping score, suspicious of others' motives, often openly resentful. Charlie found that he now looked for opportunities to be away from her, even though that also meant he was away from Ryan. Heather had started using Ryan as leverage to keep him closer to home. He suspected that her volatility was really a deep-seated cry for attention, but he feared that any show of vulnerability would be perceived by her as a final opportunity to receive the "payback" of missing love and affection that he had withheld over the years. Charlie thought about the perfect father-daughter relationship between Jenny and their father. After divorce and God knows what else, James had found love and purpose and nurtured it in the constant reaffirmation of Jenny's presence. There was no conflict in their relationship except that they were apart for long periods of time when James was in Vancouver.

Charlie could tell that the abduction theory was gaining credibility with James, and that he would defend him from any misguided conclusions from the RMCP. As they sat down to dinner he reached across the table and held Charlie's hand.

"Father, for this food, for our family, and especially for your protection for Jenny, we pray now together in Christ's name. Amen."

Charlie couldn't remember the last time he had said grace before a meal, but in this context it seemed completely reasonable that they would offer a prayer for Jenny's safety. After grace, the two men sat across from one another and silently enjoyed their chicken. Charlie sensed that the ritual of the evening meal was causing James to miss Jenny, and he decided to break the silence.

"Tell me about Victoria House."

"French toast and clean sheets."

"Sounds ideal."

"Everyone gets clean sheets on their first night, and every morning we serve French toast."

"How many can you accommodate?"

"Normally thirty, but when it gets below freezing we've had over fifty."

Charlie could see that James started to relax when he talked about his work, so he kept going. "How does someone find out you're there?"

"The police know about us, but mostly it's word-of-mouth. We get people from all over—every life circumstance. What they have in common is that they are out of money and in need of a place to stay and something to eat. We try to give preference to single moms, especially ones with little kids, but our policy is that no one stays beyond a week. We're in a network of halfway houses throughout western Canada. If people request it, we help them find a place for longer term. Rob Curtin and I run the day-to-day operations, but there are also volunteers who do everything from helping to cook breakfast to spending hours in the laundry. Clean sheets are a big deal to someone who has been sleeping in a worn-out blanket or in the back of a car."

Having his father sitting across from him made Charlie want to be completely honest, and he thought about telling him about the bathtub moments with Jenny. It seemed a little incongruent with the rest of his story, and he wasn't sure how James might react to the image of him in the bathroom with Jenny naked in the tub. He didn't want to compromise James's pristine image of Jenny, so he concluded that leaving out this insignificant detail would be the prudent course of action.

"Did you finish your report?" James began to clear the table and to put the dishes in the sink.

"Let me do the dishes. Sounds like you do your own share of dishes in Vancouver." Charlie wanted to do something for his dad, and since he arrived, James had been doing all the work. "I'll finish the report in the morning. While I do the dishes, why don't you get some rest?"

"Are you sleeping in Jenny's room?"

Charlie had not even considered where he would sleep once James arrived, but it was either Jenny's room or the sofa.

"I guess I am. Is that OK?"

"She's the only one who has slept in that bed, but at least you two are related."

With that James walked over, gave Charlie a hug and headed up to bed. As he climbed the stairs, Charlie could barely hear his father's parting goodbye.

"Jenny and I are glad you're here. Get a good night's sleep."

Charlie finished the dishes, replenished the fire, and headed up to Jenny's room. As he entered it was completely dark, and Charlie felt around for a switch to the overhead light. As he flipped the switch he realized that there was not an overhead, but the switch controlled a standing lamp in the corner. Jenny's bed was unmade and her Chinese robe was draped over a chair. The entire room smelled like her; the same sweet perfume smell that still filled the bathroom. On her night table was a picture of James and her on skis with the Canadian Rockies in the background.

Charlie slid into Jenny's bed and pulled the sheet and coverlet up around him. The pillowcase smelled of her perfume, as did the entire bed. Before he turned out the light, he took her Chinese robe from the chair and carefully placed it next to his pillow. He knew that sleeping with her robe was a little odd, but he wanted the room to be filled with her presence. As he drifted off to sleep, he remembered kneeling next to her on the bathroom floor, and the way that her hair had cascaded down when she released it from the porcelain clip. Despite the fact that nothing had actually happened, it was an intimate moment, and he thought about how intimacy is enhanced by spontaneity. Intimacy with Heather had its moments of creativity, but as in many marriages, it had also become an exercise in reverting to the familiar for reasons of utility or convenience.

Despite their half sibling bond and their brief acquaintance, Jenny remained for him an exotic woman, perhaps even more so since her disappearance. Even sleeping without her in her bed provided a level of excitement that he was not able to fully comprehend or explain.

Three hours later, Charlie was awakened from a deep sleep by the sound of Jenny screaming. It was exactly the same scream he had heard on mile four of the trail, only this time it was closer and louder. He even got up and went to the window, thinking that she was in the driveway. He stood there for a minute gazing down at her car, which looked abandoned in the light snowfall.

Realizing that the scream was only in his imagination, he crawled back into bed, wrapping Jenny's robe around his neck and shoulders, and he drifted back to sleep. What happened next must have been a dream, but it was so real that Charlie thought Jenny was there with him in her bedroom.

She was standing in a small yard at a house next to a lake, and she kept pointing at two figures inside the house and covering her mouth. One side of the house had been completely torn away, so it was like a child's dollhouse with the rooms completely exposed.

One of the downstairs rooms was a kitchen, and next to it was a bathroom with a large tub. A heavyset man was in the kitchen, and at the kitchen table were two place settings. As the man prepared dinner, a figure appeared from the back of the house who also looked like Jenny wearing a Chinese robe. She spent several minutes in the bathroom filling the running bath water with oils and perfume. At intervals the man in the kitchen would open the door separating the two rooms and say something to the Jenny who was now in the bathtub. Whatever he said, the response from the Jenny in the tub was to shake her head vigorously left and right as if to give an emphatic "no."

The Jenny in the yard was covering her eyes and also shaking her head back and forth out of disgust and fear. The man in the kitchen methodically began to turn out the lights in the kitchen and the other downstairs rooms. Only the bathroom light was left on and from the outside, the bathroom appeared as a small theatre, so that the ensuing action was more focused and intensified. As the man entered the bathroom from the door to the kitchen, the Jenny in the bathtub began to scream and her screams were identical to the screaming that Charlie had heard on the trail and earlier that evening. As the screaming continued, the man moved to the far end of the tub and began to vigorously wash Jenny's hair.

At first she resisted, but as he persisted for several long minutes, she became tired and listless. Instead of stopping, he rinsed and washed it several more times, so that now she was almost unable to hold up her head. What should have been a sensual moment became a demonstration of his inability to approximate intimacy with a woman. Jenny was completely helpless as he erroneously assumed that her silence was an indication of pleasure. Her hair also now looked exhausted, and it hung over to one side in a lifeless swirl. In frustration the man gathered her up in her robe and a few towels and carried her to the kitchen. As he placed her in front of one of the place settings, the only available light was streaming into the kitchen from the bathroom. Jenny was barely able to sit up, and eventually the man used a high-back chair to prop her up on one side. He then sat across from her and began to eat his meal as he continued to stare directly at her. He was like a man who had spent his life savings on a purchase that failed to operate as he had expected. Charlie wondered if this was a nightly occurrence, a repeated action that always produced the same result. He also noticed the Jenny in the front yard, who was huddled in a ball and crying. She seemed to be the one who was allowed to express her emotions, but was trapped as the helpless observer. The Jenny in the kitchen was like a lifeless doll. The light in the bathroom suddenly went dark, and Charlie woke up clasping Jenny's Chinese robe. He was disoriented and feverish as he attempted to reassure himself that what had just occurred was a dream.

The next morning James fixed French toast for both of them, and Charlie finished his report. He wanted to share his dream with his father, but he feared that his close association with the events of last night's dream would raise additional questions. His credibility was already tenuous, and he wanted to preserve the relative normalcy that had settled in since his father had returned home.

Welcoming an RCMP detective at 9:00 A.M. on a Sunday morning seemed a strange way to begin the week, but James reasoned that if it could help to find Jenny, it was worth any inconvenience. Both James and Charlie were expecting one man to arrive, so they were both surprised when an RCMP sedan came up the driveway and two officers emerged from the car. One of them was in full uniform and the other was in a dark business suit.

James opened the front door and immediately shook their hands with Charlie just one step behind.

"Good morning, gentlemen. I'm James Monroe, and this is my son, Charlie Benjamin."

The man in the business suit spoke first.

"Good morning Mr. Monroe, Mr. Benjamin. I'm Inspector Macpherson and this is Sergeant Hardy. We understand there is a missing person."

As James invited them in, Charlie noticed that the sergeant immediately began looking around and taking brief notes on his smartphone. He also had a small pack attached to his belt with an RCMP insignia imprinted on the outside. Charlie guessed that the two of them had worked together on missing person cases in the past.

"Why don't we have the one most familiar with what actually happened give us a brief summary."

Charlie was aware that for this initial segment, they would both just listen, and he wanted his verbal report to be consistent with what he had said in writing. The sergeant in particular might notice any inconsistencies, but he noticed that the inspector pulled out a small voice recorder as he began to speak. Aside from a few interruptions when the two of them asked clarifying details, they allowed Charlie to tell his story from the time he knocked on the door just three days ago until the arrival of James late yesterday morning.

When he came to the part about Jenny going up to wash her hair, he simply said that he had done the dishes while she had bathed and later the two of them had talked by the fire. He played down the part about her negative reaction to the news that they shared the same father, and he didn't mention that she had initially asked him to leave on Friday morning. When he finished, the inspector played with his voice recorder for a few minutes, and the sergeant continued to take notes on his phone. Neither of them said a word. Finally the inspector looked up and addressed Charlie.

"Mr. Benjamin, is it possible that you've left out some important detail, some small occurrence that could also be helpful as we investigate?"

It occurred to Charlie that the two of them were very astute, and they were used to hearing explanations where the narrator left out incriminating information. In other words, their question was possibly standard for this type of investigation.

"That's really all that happened. I wish there were some additional details that would help solve the case, but I've told you all I know."

The sergeant gave Charlie a quick look that said, "I know you're lying." But then Charlie thought he had just imagined the sergeant's quick judgment.

"By the way, I ran the WL license letters through the codex system at our K Division. There are thirty-six vehicles with Alberta plates that have WL as the first two letters, but only four trucks, and one of them belongs to an RCMP Superintendent, so that leaves three. I have a person in Banff tracking down the owners."

It was a random comment by the inspector, but Charlie reasoned it might have been a canard thrown into the discussion to relieve further tension about possible missing details. He was beginning to think that everything the two of them said was carefully orchestrated, and that they coordinated all of their questioning to produce the desired result.

"If you don't mind, we'd like to look around the house. You're welcome to guide us through, but our preference would be to wander freely."

"Of course, Inspector. Charlie and I will do breakfast dishes while the two of you poke around."

James made it sound like the rules of a parlor game, but as the sergeant headed up the stairs, Charlie noticed that he was removing surgical gloves from his belt pack, which could only mean the pack contained fingerprinting materials that he was about to use upstairs. Charlie watched him disappear into the bathroom and close the door.

He started into the kitchen to help with the dishes, but he had a sudden flashback to kneeling next to the tub when his father had arrived yesterday morning. He was going to wipe down around the base, but with his father's arrival, he hadn't quite finished the job. He didn't know the sergeant well, but he knew that he would be thorough in collecting fingerprints.

The two of them were in the house for another hour, taking photos with their phones, looking around the woodpile, and checking Jenny's car for fingerprints. At one point, the sergeant spent at least fifteen minutes in the front seat of his car, talking to someone on the radio, and Charlie suspected that he was doing a background check on the Illinois plates on his own car. The inspector eventually joined the sergeant, and the two of them sat in the driveway talking for another fifteen minutes before coming back inside.

With all four men now standing in the front hallway, the inspector was the first to speak, and he directed his question at James.

"Could you give us an article of Jenny's clothing that would be sure to have her scent? We often use trained dogs in these investigations, and we need something that she often wears."

"That would be her Chinese robe. She wears it all the time. Let me run up and find it."

As James headed up the stairs, all of the blood drained out of Charlie's face. He was grasping for what to say and what he said sounded completely ridiculous.

"I've heard that socks or stockings are the best clothing to hold a scent."

The inspector and the sergeant stood in silence, not even favoring Charlie's assertion with a reply, so that the three of them stood together without saying a word.

James walked down the stairs. He had placed the robe in a large plastic bag, and he handed it to the inspector.

"The sergeant and I were also hoping to see your driver's licenses and to take your fingerprints. The fingerprint part will save us quite a bit of time as we won't have to first figure out your prints before distinguishing them from a stranger's prints. We also need a piece of your clothing for the same reason."

Charlie had a vague recollection that you would have to be arrested before fingerprints could be legally taken, but his father was already nodding a "yes" that a license check and fingerprints would be fine. Charlie knew that to give any pushback while his father was being so compliant would look suspicious, so he handed the sergeant his license and the same winter scarf he had worn on the trail while the inspector prepared to get their prints.

While the fingerprinting was going on, the sergeant returned to the sedan with their licenses and again spent another fifteen minutes on the radio. Charlie felt like he had been caught in a speed trap, and all of this personal history was being fed to the sergeant by a computer in Edmonton.

They had barely asked about the man in the truck, and Charlie began to feel like they had a hunch that he had something to do with Jenny's disappearance. Just as it seemed that they had completed this phase of the investigation, the sergeant returned from the sedan and asked for a few minutes alone with the inspector.

When they returned to the front hallway, the sergeant cleared his throat and looked at Charlie.

"May I ask you one more rather personal question?"

Charlie's mind raced ahead, trying to imagine what was coming. The sergeant didn't wait for Charlie's reply.

"Since your arrival on Thursday, have you only taken showers or have you also had a bath?"

"I actually took a bath yesterday morning." Charlie was making it up as he went along. "Normally I take showers, but I was trying to get myself settled down after the trauma of Jenny's disappearance. Also it reminded me of her."

As soon as Charlie said "reminded me of her," he regretted it.

"How was a bath a reminder of her?"

The sergeant's quick response came as he was still taking notes on his phone.

"I just meant that I knew she liked to take baths." Now it was becoming a cross-examination.

"But you had only known her for less than a day."

At that the inspector decided to interrupt the sergeant, as he sensed that they were pursuing only a speculative line of questioning.

"I just wanted to mention to Mr. Benjamin that he should plan to remain in Alberta for a while until we can begin to sort this out."

The inspector had left his statement intentionally ambiguous. It was stronger than an invitation but not quite an edict.

"Of course," Charlie said. "I wasn't planning on heading back until I know Jenny is safe."

The two officers glanced at one another, said their goodbyes, and headed out to their car. Just when Charlie thought that he heard them backing down the driveway, the car stopped. The sergeant got out and came back up to the house. Charlie greeted him at the door.

"Just one more thing. Did you have occasion to use your own car since your arrival on Thursday evening?"

"It hasn't moved since I arrived."

"How about Jenny's car?"

"Nope. It's been sitting here the entire time."

As the sergeant headed back out to the sedan, Charlie remembered that he sat in Jenny's car to turn off the ignition, and so his fingerprints would be on the keys. But he had mentioned being in her car when he found her hair clip. That detail was in both the written report and in the oral summary. Still, with his prints on the steering wheel and on the keys, they might hypothesize that he had used her car to dispose of her body and that he had made up the hair clip story as a cover. Why else would the sergeant have come back up the driveway to clarify the use of the cars?

While James prepared to go back into the village to ask others about the mystery truck, Charlie sat next to the fire and again contemplated his situation.

The police now had Jenny's Chinese robe, and it would only be a number of hours before they discovered that it was covered with his fingerprints. The sergeant had scoured the bathroom for fingerprints, and he had undoubtedly discovered something around the base of the tub, which prompted his inquiry about showering versus bathing.

How would he possibly explain the fingerprints on Jenny's robe to his father? How would he explain such a thing to Heather? Charlie thought back to his long nap the previous afternoon. He had felt safe and protected, confident that his father would sort out Jenny's disappearance. Now, in a matter of hours, he had become the chief suspect in the case, and he had been told by the RCMP not to leave Canada. He would have to call his office and Heather in less than twenty-four hours with the Monday morning news that he would have to remain in Alberta.

Worse, he would have to tell James about his fingerprints on the robe. If he wanted his father's care and support, he would have to tell him about sleeping with the robe. And this would prompt his father to wonder what else he had failed to tell him. And finally, he knew that the inspector and the sergeant would be back, and they would become even more suspicious when they discovered that he had changed his story and was the type of suspect who was unreliable and adept at lying.

CHAPTER THIRTEEN

GERARD HUGEL RANG UP OUR ROOM AT THE NORFOLK shortly before noon, and Melissa headed down to the lobby for their extended lunch date. Before she walked out of the door, she gave me one of her "everything will be fine" kisses, which doubled as both a reassurance of her "business only" intentions with Gerard as well as a "good luck with your lunch" send-off. She was always able to communicate her "don't let me down" expectations with only a few words, or in this case, with only a kiss and three seconds of eye contact.

When I arrived on the Lord Delamere Terrace a few minutes later, I found Nisar Malik sitting at the same table that Melissa, Gerard, and I had occupied the evening before, and as soon as I saw him, I realized that we had met several years ago at a World Bank meeting at the Taj Mahal Palace Hotel in Bombay.

At that time he was heading up the roads and highways construction division for all Indian government projects in the Maharashtra State, and the World Bank had been an ongoing partner in the new road construction south of Bombay. I remembered him as a tough negotiator, but there was a question at the Bank as to whether he was part of the corruption problem in Bombay, or a person who would be integral to the project's successful execution. He may have been a little of both.

"Good to see you, Nisar."

He half rose from his chair to greet me and at the same time extinguished his Gold Flake, which had only been smoked a third of the way down.

"Mr. Monroe. We met a few years ago in Bombay."

"And my colleague, David Fortran, tells me there has been yet another contract that has fallen through."

The waiter came by to fill water glasses and to give us menus. Nisar said something to him in Hindi and he removed the menus and returned to the waiter station.

"Aren't we going to eat lunch?"

"Of course we are, but I wanted thirty minutes of uninterrupted time so that I can tell you what is really going on in Bombay."

"I thought you were no longer with the government."

"That's correct. I resigned fourteen months ago. But I've gotten back into it as a consultant."

"A consultant to what? Further corruption?"

Nisar pushed back his chair and lit another cigarette.

"The word is out that the Bank is about to pull the plug on further funding. It's finally a wake-up call to the ministry in Bombay that has already received 400,000 INR in kickbacks from potential contractors. They won't make a contract decision, because now there are death threats from the contractors who have already paid but won't be given the project. The ministry is in paralysis because without Bank funding, they can't underwrite the project, and they certainly can't pay bank monies already received from potential contractors. Those funds have essentially disappeared. The ministry is blaming the World Bank based on the funding delays, but there are layers of corruption that will take decades to sort out, and that will open the door for the Ministry of Transportation to be replaced by a private corporation."

"A private corporation that hired you?"

"Actually, I was hired by a group of investors."

Nisar motioned the waiter to return and he ordered two beers, this time in English.

"Would the Indian government replace an entire ministry with a private corporation?"

"There are ways to do it that would leave the ministry as a shell entity, in other words, as a front for the privately owned and controlled corporation."

The beers arrived with two glasses and Nisar poured one for himself and one for me. We lightly tapped glasses; he paused and lit yet another cigarette. I guessed what was coming next.

"We think you may be able to help us with the transition from state-controlled to privately owned. After all, isn't that a mission of the World Bank?"

Nisar was correct that one of the Bank's goals was to move third world countries from government-controlled economies to a privatized free enterprise model, but the methods were always transparent, not a manipulation that would intentionally bankrupt a particular government ministry.

"What are you asking me to do?"

"All we're asking is that you and your associates at the Bank speed up the process of withdrawing funding."

He kept using the plural "we," as if the group of investors were seated just behind him.

"That's a decision that others at the Bank will make. I'm no longer a part of that division."

"Still, you have associates who are involved. Specifically, Mr. David Fortran."

"You want me to talk to Fortran about tilting a Bank decision?"

"Of course there would be certain benefits for both of you."

The waiter returned with the menus and Nisar ordered another beer. I couldn't believe that I was being subjected to a scheme that involved bribery.

"If you are asking me to entertain the idea of accepting a bribe, the answer is a definitive no."

I thought about just getting up and abruptly ending the meeting.

"Do you have any idea the kind of money we are talking about?" Before I could answer, he continued on. "For all you know Mr. Fortran will tell you that the decision has already been made. Then all you would do is report back to me and receive the gratitude of all involved."

We finally ordered, and I thought about Melissa flirting her way through lunch with Gerard. The thought did flash through my mind that a windfall of cash would be another way to win her over, but I caught myself before allowing this idea to gain any credibility.

"Look, can't you just talk to Fortran and get a sense of the current status of the Bank's commitment? You know, find which way the wind is blowing?"

"If I do talk to David Fortran, it will only be to get information. I wouldn't even consider trying to influence him or the Bank's decision."

As our sandwiches arrived, Nisar leaned back in his chair. By my agreeing to at least talk to David Fortran, he knew that he had gained a small victory and something to report back to the investors. We both knew that my small concession did not deserve the kind of payoff that he had alluded to earlier, but still I sensed that he wanted to reciprocate in some way.

"That's very noble of you, James. Surely there must be some small way that I could return your kindness."

He was trying to restore some high-mindedness to the conversation by mentioning kindness and nobility, but we both knew that what had transpired was a negotiation and not an act of charity. Still, this was my opportunity to mention Jonathan Samuel.

"I'm in need of some information as well. A friend of mine has a brother who is awaiting trial in Bombay on drug smuggling charges. He has been incarcerated for almost three years, and nothing is happening."

Nisar pushed his plate away and lit yet another cigarette. He ran his right hand through his jet-black hair and exhaled in segments as if he were punctuating what he was about to say. He was now completely in his element.

"There are one or two judges in Bombay who we could convince to get him released." Nisar paused and looked out across the terrace. "But it will take a small fortune to get it done."

Nisar sensed that he had finally found the pulse that he had been searching for since we sat down to lunch. His mind was clicking ahead as to how he could use my request to his advantage with the World Bank funding proposal, and he was being careful not to appear overly anxious to connect the two.

"How much is a small fortune?"

Nisar knew that I was taking the bait, but he wanted the hook to lodge in my mouth as deeply as possible before he began to reel me in.

"You're dealing with Indian magistrates—some of whom have been on the bench for decades. They would be accepting a payoff at considerable risk to their own careers."

"Wouldn't David Fortran and I incur the same risk for manipulating a Bank decision?"

"This is different. They would leave the bench in disgrace, and they would disgrace their family name."

"How is it different?"

"The two of you would simply be moving a decision along that has essentially already been made. A judge in Bombay would be violating the entire Indian criminal justice system."

"I still don't see the difference, if you look at it as a violation of principle."

"Then why do you ask for a figure?"

"I'm hypothetically curious as to what it would cost."

"At least $25,000 US and maybe $50,000. It would depend on the judge and the circumstances. A person going into that situation would want even more than fifty in case minds began to change at the last moment. Coincidentally, $50,000 US is what the investors had in mind for both you and David Fortran if you were willing to help us out."

"Now our conversation has shifted from bribery to blackmail?"

"Give it any name you wish. In my mind, we are completing a business transaction."

"A few minutes ago you were talking about kindness and nobility."

"And since you are checking on the status of the Bank's commitment, I will do something for you. There are two judges in Bombay City who are brothers. One of them—I will get you his name and contact information—has been known to accept payments to either commute sentences or dismiss charges altogether. The other brother is known as one of the harshest magistrates in all of Maharashtra State."

"How does one go about contacting a judge?"

"You have to know someone in government."

"I have World Bank connections in Bombay, but they are all in the financial sector."

Our waiters cleared the plates and without asking, brought us coffee.

"She's very beautiful."

"Who?"

"Your wife."

"You mean Melissa. When did you meet her?"

"I saw her in the lobby just a few minutes before I sat down on the terrace."

"How did you know she was my wife?"

"She was with another man, but I asked the concierge who she was and he said 'Mrs. Monroe from Room 17.' The other man, by the way, seemed very interested."

I realized that I had been sitting with Nisar for almost two hours, and I wondered what Melissa and Gerard were doing at that very moment.

"Do you always allow your wife to go off with such handsome men?"

Little did Nisar know that he was striking a chord that could move me one step closer to accepting his offer.

As we sat across from each other, I didn't reveal any vulnerability, but silently I was calculating where I might come up with $25,000, or perhaps $50,000, to rescue Jonathan. I had $30,000 of my own money in a bank in New York, but that was Jenny's money for her final two years of college. Using it for some other purpose could jeopardize her education. But taking money to influence a Bank decision was equally repugnant.

What I did know was Nisar could open doors for me in Bombay, and I didn't know anyone else with those credentials. My plan for the moment was to keep him at bay until I could gather additional information, and then extricate myself when I saw the right opportunity.

It sounded innocuous, but later, when this strategy completely backfired, I looked back at our lunch on the terrace as the beginning of a series of events that turned the next nine months into a living nightmare.

CHAPTER FOURTEEN

JAMES RETURNED MIDAFTERNOON FROM HIS VILLAGE excursion and went straight into the kitchen to boil water for tea. While he was away, Charlie had attempted to sleep on the sofa; he didn't want to nap on James's bed, and Jenny's room now seemed completely off limits. He had no idea where he would sleep that evening.

Without even asking Charlie, James fixed tea for both of them and they sat across from each other in the chairs next to the fireplace. James could see that Charlie was feeling uncomfortable, and he allowed him to begin the conversation.

"How was the village?"

"I sat in the diner for a few hours, listening in on the local gossip. If someone saw something, it will eventually surface among the locals."

"Shouldn't we be doing more than eavesdropping in the diner? Jenny has now been gone for over forty-eight hours, and we don't even have a lead."

"That's what we're looking for, a lead."

"The inspector and the sergeant seemed pretty casual about the license plate lead."

"It's the weekend. They won't run the plate numbers completely until tomorrow morning."

The two of them sat quietly staring into the fire and sipping tea. Charlie knew that this would be the ideal opportunity to tell James the truth, but he continued to hesitate. It was James who spoke first.

"What did you think of those two?"

"The sergeant seemed overly aggressive."

"How was he aggressive?"

"All that fingerprinting. He must have covered every inch of the upstairs."

"Just doing his job. If it helps us to find Jenny, it will all be worth it."

"I'm worried about what he may have found upstairs."

James put down his teacup and looked directly at his son.

"What are you worried about?"

Charlie realized that the moment had arrived, and he closed his eyes for about twenty seconds as if he were trying to remember exactly what happened. He didn't want to look directly at James, so as he began to speak, he gazed into the fire.

"After dinner on Thursday evening, Jenny asked if I could bring her phone to the bathroom as she prepared to wash her hair. She was already in the tub when I opened the door. At one point I knelt next to her as I attempted to find the shampoo, which had slipped under the tub. It was an intimate moment but obviously nothing happened. But because of the shampoo my fingerprints were all over the outside of the tub. I should have mentioned this earlier, but when she joined me downstairs and we had cognac by the fire, I told her that we both had the same father."

James's expression had not changed at all, and now both men sat staring into the fire.

"Is there some other reason why you are worried about the sergeant's extensive fingerprint search?"

Charlie was encouraged by James's neutral acceptance of the hair interlude; he decided to also mention the Chinese robe.

"Last night when I slept in Jenny's room, I put her robe next to me in bed. I wanted something that would remind me of her. During the night I heard her screaming. It was so real that I actually went to the window to see if she was in the driveway. When I returned to bed, I had a dream that she was bathing and her abductor was attempting to wash her hair, hoping that it would result in sexual intimacy. The house was on a lake, and there was a second Jenny standing in the yard and crying as she observed what was occurring in the house. When I awakened, Jenny's robe was wrapped around my neck, so if the RCMP uses dogs, my scent will be all over her robe."

Both men sat in silence; the only sound the cracking and popping of the fire. James deliberately waited a few minutes before he spoke.

"Of course I believe you, and I thank you for your honesty. The hair sequence will be easy enough to explain. It's not so unusual to ask another person to help while you are in the bathtub. The problem with the robe explanation is that it has too many moving parts. They will, of course, assume that you slept with her, and the scent on the robe is evidence that whether she wanted you in her bed or not, enough went on for your fingerprints and scent to be all over the robe. They might speculate that many homicides begin with sexual encounters that turn violent, even though you may not have any violent sexual history. They may want to depose your wife, and they may ask her very difficult questions regarding your sexual behavior and any sudden inexplicable mood changes on your part. That would require her to be very candid and very careful about how she phrases things."

Charlie listened in dead silence. His fate could now be partially in Heather's hands. She could easily use the opportunity to get back at him. For all she knew, he had lied about not sleeping with Jenny, and then something had happened. Either Jenny had left in disgust or Charlie had found a way to keep her quiet. Either way, Charlie thought about Heather's propensity to become prosecutorial. Her new plan might be to put him behind bars and for her and Ryan to begin a new life together with a man who would be trustworthy and responsible.

"How do you know so much about what the RCMP will assume?"

"We have people show up at Victoria House who have had all sorts of scrapes with the law. Part of their healing is to be able to talk to someone who is nonjudgmental. Some try to hide the lives they have left behind; others need to talk to keep their sanity. So we give them food, a place to sleep, and (if they ask) even a little therapy."

"How can I soften the blow of this with the RCMP?"

"We need to call the inspector and tell him we have additional information. They probably won't discover the scent and fingerprints until Monday or Tuesday. It will be much better if they hear the truth from us instead of reading it on a forensics report."

"Won't they still assume that it's an alibi?"

"Probably, but at least we will have a fighting chance. We need to get the inspector on our side. The sergeant is probably a lost cause. What we need is some evidence that points to the mechanic."

"How about Jenny's phone?"

"The sergeant put it in his belt pack. He said something about also needing a password, but I don't think her phone is password protected."

"Instead of giving it to the sergeant, we should have driven it to Edmonton. Some techie could have gotten into the call history. If the sergeant has already decided that I'm the only valid suspect, he may not go out of his way to chase down other leads."

"There are scores of innocent men and women who are sitting

in prison because some district attorney wanted another notch in his belt. False accusations have a way of gathering their own momentum."

"So should I call the inspector?"

"Let me call him first thing in the morning. You have to respect his privilege of having one day a week to spend with his family."

Charlie remembered that he would also be calling Heather and his office the next morning to tell them that he was required by the RCMP to remain in Canada, so now he felt as if his entire life was pivoting toward tragedy.

That evening, Charlie barely touched the casserole that James made for dinner, and as the house darkened, Charlie sat paralyzed next to the fire. He was not only in danger of losing his job and his family; he was in danger of being arrested for a crime that he did not commit. By his own fault, the circumstantial evidence was mounting against him, and despite his father's ongoing support, he couldn't imagine a sequence of events that would return him to the normal existence he had enjoyed just a week ago.

The thought of spending the night on the sofa held little appeal. He was already emotionally exhausted, and he desperately needed a good night's sleep. He was hesitant to return to Jenny's bed, since his sleeping there last night had caused his own incrimination, but despite that hesitancy, he headed up the stairs to her room, rationalizing that the damage had already been done.

Her robe was no longer there, but her pillows and sheets still smelled of her, and as he removed his clothes and slipped under the sheets, a great sadness engulfed him. He was sad for his own situation, but the smell of her reminded him that she was out there somewhere, perhaps dead, but just as likely still alive and feeling frightened and alone. As Charlie drifted off to sleep, he also thought of Heather and Ryan. He knew that despite her bravado, Heather was also feeling lonely and afraid. Charlie imagined Ryan clutching one of his stuffed animals, wondering when his father would return. It was all a little too much, and when sleep finally did arrive, he embraced its quiet oblivion as a last refuge before the storm.

Several hours later, Charlie was awakened from a dead sleep by the sound of his own name.

"Charlie."

The voice saying his name was distinctive and feminine. For a moment he thought it was Jenny. But the image appearing just next to the bed was not his sister; rather, it was his mother.

Charlie knew immediately that it was Teresa, because as he was opening his eyes, she again repeated his name, and she gave him one of her broad and welcoming smiles. She looked remarkably younger. Charlie immediately thought of the pictures he had seen of her when she was in her mid-twenties, and she was dressed in typical Teresa style: silk scarf, hair clips, collar up in the back.

"Charlie. All will be well."

It was one short sentence as she began to evaporate into the darkness, but it was said with such clarity and conviction that it immediately filled him with the same sense of assurance that Teresa was able to give him when she was alive. Teresa always had a way of coming to the rescue, and she did it in a way that seemed unrehearsed and effortless. Her sure confidence alone was always able to stem the tide.

Charlie lay staring into the darkness for the next thirty minutes. His mother had died five months ago, and yet she had just been in the room, larger than life, to comfort her son. Charlie had this crazy idea that she may have also appeared to James, since they didn't have a chance to say goodbye before she died. He thought about going into James's room to tell him about her apparition, but he reconsidered when he thought about his tenuous credibility regarding the night visit of the mechanic. James might begin to think that he had a difficult time distinguishing between fantasy and reality.

Still, Teresa's appearance and her hopeful message had a

profoundly positive effect on Charlie, and he fell fast asleep until a little after dawn, when he heard his father head down the stairs to the kitchen.

After breakfast, James took his phone and went out to the driveway to call the inspector. When he returned, he seemed subdued and distracted.

"How did the call go?"

Charlie was still cleaning up from breakfast and rehearsing his call to the office. He had already decided that the office call should precede his call to Heather.

"The inspector said that if any of your original report has changed, you should write it down and they will take a look when they return on Wednesday. He seemed very businesslike on the phone."

"Did he say anything else?"

"He asked me if I would be willing to take on the responsibility of being sure you remained in Alberta."

"I told them yesterday that I wouldn't leave. Why all the formality?"

"He mentioned that they would get fingerprint results by tomorrow afternoon and that they would share them with us on Wednesday."

"So there is also at least a chance that the phone will give them the call history by Wednesday?"

"He didn't mention the phone."

"But the phone is the best chance of proving his guilt."

"Phone calls back and forth wouldn't necessarily lead to an abduction."

"But at least the man could be found and questioned."

"Maybe. He could always have been using a throwaway cell phone."

"That would have involved quite a bit of planning. I think the abduction was something he dreamed up that morning. Did the inspector say anything else?"

"He asked me to get your car keys."

"What?"

"It's just a precaution on their part."

"For all they know I could walk down to the village and get on a train."

"True. But from their perspective the convenience of just getting in your car and driving away would no longer be an option."

"Shouldn't I get an attorney?"

"Let's wait until Wednesday and see what they have to say. If you get an attorney now, it may make you look more culpable."

James decided that to talk anymore about it was just making Charlie feel worse. He wasn't going to demand the keys, but he felt better when Charlie quietly left the keys on the kitchen table. James's philosophy since India had been "the less said, the better," and so he intentionally wanted normalcy to return despite Jenny's disappearance and Charlie's cloud of suspicion. His job as a father was to keep things on an even keel in spite of deteriorating outward circumstances.

The morning had not been the ideal preamble for calls to Williston, Hughes and Meyers, or Heather, but Charlie knew he had no choice. As he dialed the office, he hoped that Todd Hughes would be available since Todd liked him and always gave him the benefit of the doubt. The person he wanted to avoid at all costs was Craig. Craig was undoubtedly keeping track of every call Charlie had missed from a client as well as every unreturned email. Craig envied Charlie's position as a partner, and he celebrated when Charlie did something that might jeopardize client relations. As he dialed the number, he realized that it was nearing the lunch hour in Chicago.

"Williston, Hughes and Meyers."

"Hi, Diane. It's Charlie. Is Todd around?"

"Todd is having lunch with clients. Do you want his voicemail?"

"How about Bill Meyers? Is he also at lunch?"

"I think Bill just finished a meeting in the conference room. I'll try over there."

"Conference room; this is Craig Ela."

"Hey Craig. It's Charlie. Is Bill around?"

"Bill is in Todd's office, signing papers. Are you finally back?"

"Not yet. I should be back by Wednesday, Thursday at the latest."

"Hey, while I have you on the phone, you've missed a ton of client calls. When I talked to Heather, she said you'd be home by Saturday, so I wasn't that worried. Thursday? Really? I tried to forward the voicemails to your cell phone but your mailbox was full. Do you want me to listen to the calls and get back to them? I know Todd would be shocked if he knew that client calls were not being returned."

"Craig, when I get off this call I will clear my mailbox and you can forward them to my cell. How's everything else going?"

"Todd and Bill were beyond upset that the contract deadline with Overton expired. We lost two hundred grand overnight. I know that Overton was not your client, but it was like a morgue around here last Friday."

"Yeah, I've had a few difficult days out here as well."

"Oh, is your brother-in-law still having a tough time?"

Charlie didn't want to perpetuate the brother-in-law story even though he ostensibly went to western Canada to help Heather's brother. Mostly he wanted to end the call with Craig.

"Listen Craig, speaking of my brother-in-law, I need to meet him in a few minutes. Tell Todd that I called and I'll check in on Wednesday."

As Charlie hung up the phone, he couldn't imagine how long he could keep up the charade of being "almost home." His office had an above average tolerance for family emergencies, but when business was being impacted, it could go quickly downhill.

Worse than talking to Craig would be the call to Heather. Her parting words in their last conversation had amounted to a request for a trial separation. As he dialed her cell phone, he didn't know if she would even talk to him.

"Hello."

"Heather, it's Charlie."

"I know. I saw it on the caller ID."

Neither of them spoke for about twenty seconds.

"So why did you call?"

"I called because I felt bad about the way our last call ended."

"Talk is cheap, Charlie. If you really felt bad about the call, you'd be home by now."

"I've actually been advised by the Royal Canadian Mounted Police that I cannot leave Canada until the thing with Jenny gets sorted out."

"You've been 'advised.' What does that mean, 'you've been advised'?"

"It means that I cannot leave here, and the timeframe is indeterminate."

"What did you do to her? You lied to me. You slept with her, didn't you, Charlie? You slept with her and then what? Did you get mad and do something stupid?"

"I didn't sleep with her, but there is some bogus circumstantial evidence that is not working in my favor."

Charlie could hear Heather put the phone down, and he could hear Ryan in the background.

"Here, Charlie. I don't want to talk to you. You are a lying, unfaithful bastard. So if you want to call here in the future, I don't want to talk to you. But Ryan misses you and he wants to say hello to his father."

"Hi Dad."

"Hey Flyin' Ryan, how's everything going?"

"I miss you, Dad."

"Hey buddy, I miss you to the moon and back. I'm hoping I'll be home soon."

"Will you be here for my soccer game?"

"Maybe not for your Thursday night game, but we'll see."

"Thursday night is father-son night."

Charlie could barely speak but he knew that he had to stay upbeat for his son.

"Hey, when I get home, every game night will be a father-son night."

"Ok, Dad."

Charlie could hear the disappointment in Ryan's voice.

"I love you Ryan."

"I love you too, Dad." Charlie saw "call ended" appear on his phone. Ryan either ended the call or he handed the phone to Heather and instead of saying goodbye, she simply hung up.

"How did your calls go?"

James had his coat on and Charlie wasn't sure if he was headed out or had just returned.

"Not great. The one with Heather was particularly volatile."

"May I give you some fatherly advice?"

"Anything would be helpful at this point."

"Stay focused on your son. Be more proactive. You might call him at the end of the school day or after a game. Let him know that while you are here in Alberta, you still want to support him and be a part of his life. With Heather, be brutally honest and ask for her forgiveness. Let her know that you care for her despite all that has happened. She may be volatile, but there is a part of her that desperately wants your marriage to work. Agree with her and don't be adversarial. You will notice how the whole dynamic will change."

"And what about the office? How should I handle things?"

"Call the partner who you trust the most, and again be brutally honest. If you are honest with people, they are willing to accept almost anything. Any lying or cover-up will work against you in the end. And do whatever work you can by phone or email to stay current. If I were you, I would call the office every day."

Just listening to James's calm and clear direction was like a balm for Charlie. Of course there were solutions to each of his problems, and James had a way of offering very specific directions of what he should do next. Charlie remembered that Craig was going to forward voicemails. He quickly cleared his voice mailbox and texted Craig that he could go ahead with the forwarding.

Redirecting his focus to work-related issues helped Charlie regain some perspective, and he used the next forty-eight hours to reassert his stature at the firm. He still had not spoken to Todd, but he wanted that conversation to be interspersed with his accurate observations of how things were progressing with clients.

James seemed pleased to see Charlie so motivated, so he decided not to mention that the inspector had called to arrange a 10:00 A.M. meeting at the house on Wednesday.

This time two RCMP vehicles arrived, a sedan and a small van. The inspector and the sergeant emerged from the sedan, and a fully uniformed Mountie got out of the van. James noticed a pair of handcuffs dangling from the Mountie's side. Charlie was resting in Jenny's room, and as the men strode across the driveway, James called up to him to come down.

In the doorway, brief introductions were made, and James invited the three men to sit by the fire. All three seemed particularly formal, and after everyone was seated, the inspector was the first to speak.

"Quite a bit has transpired since our visit on Sunday, and both of you are entitled to know where things stand."

Charlie noticed that the Mountie with the handcuffs would only look at the inspector. The sergeant looked down at the floor.

"On Sunday afternoon after we left here, we went to talk with your neighbors. We won't mention any names, but one of them remembered seeing Miss Monroe's black Saab pulling out of the driveway late Thursday afternoon, and a man who they didn't recognize was driving."

"That was the mechanic driving. He was probably testing out the new relay."

Charlie's outburst seemed incongruous with the calm demeanor of the inspector, and instead of responding to Charlie, he quietly continued.

"When we were here last Sunday, the sergeant found duct tape and scissors stuffed under the front seat. And Mr. Benjamin's fingerprints were all over the driver's side of the car."

James had listened to so many stories of false accusations while at Victoria House, he felt compelled to jump in.

"Inspector, so far what you are describing is circumstantial evidence. I think we need to be careful about jumping to conclusions."

"If you'll let me continue, Mr. Monroe, I think you will see that this goes well beyond a few circumstantial facts."

He paused to allow the next bit of evidence to sink in.

"The sergeant also found Mr. Benjamin's fingerprints all over the outside of the bathtub and even underneath the clawfoot tub. It seems more than plausible that he placed an object under the tub and groped around for it—possibly to use against Miss Monroe."

"I was helping her to find the shampoo! Look in my revised report. She asked me to help her as she washed her hair!"

The inspector completely disregarded this second outburst from Charlie, and instead cooly turned the page of his notebook.

"And then, of course, the scent from Mr. Benjamin's scarf matched the scent on her robe, and the robe was covered with his fingerprints."

"You will see in my revised report that I admit that I slept with her robe, but that happened two nights ago, not while she was still here."

Charlie looked over at the sergeant and noticed a faint smile that was one of amusement and disdain. For the first time, the inspector was going to respond to one of Charlie's comments.

"Are you accustomed to sleeping with the robe of someone you just met?"

"We had just met, but she is my half sister."

The three officers just sat there for a moment, allowing the incredulity of Charlie's last statement to fully sink in. Then the inspector asked the sergeant and the Mountie to join him in the entryway. After a few minutes, the inspector came back in and asked James to join them. The inspector spoke to James as if he were the parent of a truant schoolboy.

"We're going to have to place him in custody until we can bring the forensic evidence to a judge. If I had to predict, I'd say we will get it to a magistrate by week's end. While we are in this transition, you may want to get him an attorney. We'll have him spend the night at our facility in Banff, then he will be remanded to our Correctional Center in Edmonton to await arraignment and a trial. Because he's a non-resident of Canada, it's unlikely they'll grant him bail. Any questions?"

"Couldn't he just stay home tonight and I could drive him to Banff once we get the judge's decision?"

"Now that he knows the evidence we have compiled against him, he becomes more of a flight risk. If he happened to make it back to the States, it could take years of extradition hearings to get him back for a trial."

"Can you give me the phone numbers of the RCMP facility in Banff and the correctional facility in Edmonton?"

"Sure, the sergeant can get you these numbers. It's probably time that we get Mr. Benjamin into the van."

Charlie now appeared in the hallway. James walked over and gave him a hug. As he did, both of them winced and James whispered into Charlie's ear.

"I had to go through something similar when I was your age; only I was guilty and you are an innocent man. We will get through this together, I promise. I love you, Charlie."

"Thanks, Dad. I love you too."

The Mountie approached Charlie and asked him to raise his

arms. After frisking him, he started to put on the handcuffs, but the inspector interceded.

"We won't need the cuffs. Put him in the back of the sedan, and we'll drive him down to Banff."

Was it possible that the inspector had an intuitive hunch about Charlie's innocence? James wasn't sure, but as he watched his son being loaded into the back of a police car, all of the anguish of incarceration came rushing back to him. He thought about the night Charlie had been conceived, and all that had happened since then. He promised himself that he would not allow Charlie to endure what he had endured earlier. He would somehow save his son from that horrific reality, even if it meant losing his own life in the process.

CHAPTER FIFTEEN

Melissa didn't arrive back at the Norfolk until almost 4:00 p.m., and of course I was curious about what she and Gerard had been doing together since her noon departure.

"He knows more people in Nairobi than I know on the entire Australian continent."

In typical Melissa style, she didn't provide any specifics about her whereabouts, preferring instead to leave me with the supposition that they had spent the entire four hours meeting a small army of Gerard's friends. I had learned not to press her on the specifics, as that could potentially bring us back around to an attempt to bring definition to the parameters of our relationship, and all of those conversations had ended badly.

She, however, assumed that she was perfectly within her rights to question me about my lunch with Nisar, and she didn't hesitate to get to the specifics.

"What did he say about our chances of bribing someone to get Jonathan out of Bombay?"

"It wouldn't be impossible; in fact, Nisar might be able to introduce me to the right people. The big item would be the cost. He's estimating at least $25,000 and maybe $50,000 US."

Melissa was undressing to get into the shower, and as I said the amount, she carefully removed her bra so that now her breasts and lovely torso were in full view.

"You know that I would pay you back. Gerard has all but offered me a job, so I could save $25,000 fairly easily in six months to a year. I could even sign something if that will make you feel better."

"There's no need to sign anything. I know you will pay me back. It will take me a few days to have the money wired from my bank in New York."

As she had done on so many other occasions, Melissa rewarded my financial largesse by walking across the room to kiss me on the lips. Because she was half naked, she allowed her entire upper body to press into mine, and I thought of my negotiating disadvantage of making these arrangements while she was being so seductive.

I had allowed her to believe that I was a man of more than adequate financial means, so little did she know that I had a total in savings of $30,000, and that money was to be used for Jenny's college. Even if Melissa did pay me back in six months or a year, it would be too late to meet tuition deadlines.

Jenny was depending on that money, and as a part of the divorce settlement, I had agreed to pay for Jenny's college. So using that money to free Jonathan would be tantamount to me breaking a legal contract. For a moment my mind went back to Nisar's proposal—$50,000 US for expediting the Bank's decision to pull the plug on the road construction project. While the ministry in Bombay might be confused by the Bank's expedited decision, it would be very difficult to connect the dots back to David Fortran or me. I decided to leave the idea on the back burner. Besides, I couldn't imagine David Fortran agreeing to a plan that would manipulate a Bank decision, even though $50,000 US could buy him countless nights in high-priced brothels throughout Africa and the Middle East.

Melissa closed the bathroom door and I heard her showering. I loved that Nisar thought she was my wife. Somehow it gave me more power and credibility that he believed I was married to a woman with Melissa's poise and beauty. Although we were only pretending, it gave me an inordinate amount of satisfaction to have her referred to as Mrs. Monroe.

As I sat there, I could hear a live band warming up on the Delamere Terrace below, and I called down to the lobby to ask if the band was for a private function or for the general clientele of the hotel.

"You are, of course, invited," came the reply from the front desk, and as I hung up the phone, it rang again. I assumed it was the front desk with more information about the band, but instead it was Nisar.

"James, is this a bad time?"

"Melissa and I are getting ready to head down to dinner. How can I help?"

"I didn't realize until a few minutes ago that the investors have moved up their meeting on Friday. They are meeting tomorrow morning."

"I thought I made it clear that I would find out from David Fortran the updated status on the project. I won't be able to get a hold of him this evening. Besides, he would find it odd that I would be contacting him after hours to get the status on a project that is no longer in my portfolio."

"But have you considered my other offer?"

Nisar was sounding a little desperate. He obviously needed more to report than just an upcoming status update. I thought about Jenny waiting tables all summer, trying in vain to come up with tuition money, and her going to Catherine to announce that I had reneged on my part of the divorce settlement.

"Tell the investors that I am considering their generous offer and will get back to them by the end of the week."

I could hear Nisar's sigh of relief through the phone.

"This is very wise business practice, James. Not only do you have a beautiful wife, you are also an astute businessman. I'll be back in Nairobi on Friday, and we can meet then to tie up the details. Have a lovely dinner, James, and give my best to Mrs. Monroe."

I put down the phone as Melissa reappeared from the bathroom.

"Who were you talking to?"

"I called the front desk to find out about the live band. If you want, we can do some dancing after dinner."

"Sounds lovely. Most men can't dance, but I am confident that you, as in everything else, will defy convention."

Melissa somehow managed to slip in yet another subtle directive regarding Jonathan even though we were talking about dancing. It was one of her "Melissa expects" moments that are accompanied by momentary eye contact as if to say, "We are on the same page." She was remarkably adept at moving from "you" to "us," and like everything else from Melissa, it was an effortless transition.

I didn't want to think about the tentative "yes" that I had given to Nisar. It was a foolish acquiescence, and one that I suspected I would live to regret. At dinner that evening, I had too many glasses of red wine, but they gave me the confidence to ask Melissa to dance despite the fact that the dance floor was empty.

Melissa was a spectacular dancer—one of those people whose kinesthetic sensibility allows them to do last-second variations and combinations that are purely intuitive and inventive. The dance floor for her was a canvas that she filled with the same stylistic flair that she utilized moving around the room at a cocktail party. It appeared that nothing was left to chance, but her fluidity of motion and her ability to anticipate what I was about to do made the entire experience creative and sensorily delightful. Mostly it was her athleticism that allowed her to appear to float to the music, and there was, of course, a charisma about it that was characteristic of everything she did.

I always looked back on that evening as the last time Melissa and I were happily together. It reminded me of our evening at Victoria Falls or on the train to Bulawayo. In all three instances we found an equilibrium, a balance, that allowed us to be more fully ourselves and more fully alive. Her secret was her ability to make anyone who was around her feel more alive. She had a positive energy flow that she was able to willfully regulate in its intensity, so that every situation, every circumstance of her life had an attractive vibrancy. To be part of that vibrancy for me became an obsession, so that I was willing to sacrifice almost anything not to lose it.

The part of Melissa that remained a mystery to me was her inability to commit to any one person. The core of that inability may have been an insecurity that she was artfully able to mask. At its worst, that insecurity may have engendered a selfishness that never allowed her to open her heart fully to another person. Melissa cared for other people, but she was unable to give freely to others without expectation of return. She was interested in philosophy, but for her it was more an intellectual exercise than a true search for the meaning of life.

The next morning I called David Fortran ostensibly to ask him about a report we had both been working on concerning capacity building in Mozambique. I decided to broach the road construction project in Bombay just so I could honestly tell Nisar that David and I had talked.

"How are things going in Bombay?"

"Do you mean the road construction project?"

"I keep hearing rumors we are pulling out."

"There's been no transparency from the transportation ministry. They keep promising the financials, but recently nothing's coming out of Bombay."

"How patient will we continue to be?"

"Hard to say. There's a big meeting in two weeks when we look at all the Bank projects in western India. We'll know more at that point."

As I hung up the phone, I realized that I essentially had no news for Nisar. I might get an update in two weeks, but knowing how slowly change of any kind occurred at the Bank, I suspected that the ministry would be granted yet another extension to deliver updates on their financials. Now the idea of getting David involved in a scheme to tilt the Bank's decision regarding the loan seemed wildly preposterous. Even if he had the influence to make such a thing occur, it was highly unlikely that he would want to get involved.

I picked up the phone and asked for an international operator. My only option at this point was to have my own $30,000 from Citibank wired to a bank in Nairobi. I thought about calling Nisar to tell him that the deal was off, but I still needed his help in arranging a meeting with a pliable judge, so I wanted to keep him thinking that I could be potentially helpful. I spent the next two days at AFREA catching up on paperwork that I should have completed two weeks ago.

On Friday morning, there was a message at the front desk at The Norfolk that Mr. Malik was hoping to meet me at noon for lunch. I was sure that Nisar had told "the investors" that he could close the deal by Friday, and he wasn't going to miss a beat. I instructed the concierge to reply to Mr. Malik in the affirmative and I headed upstairs to call Jenny. It had been over three weeks since we had talked, and I wanted to hear her voice. I knew it would be early evening in New York, which was always the best time to call.

"Hi Papa."

"How did you know it was me?"

"I saw the international number on caller ID, so who else do I know who would be calling from Africa?"

"How are you, Jenny?"

"Did you get my letter about spring break?"

"Actually no, when did you mail it?"

"Awhile ago, but I'm not sure it had enough postage to get to Africa."

"So, what's up?"

"I want to go to Sarasota with friends for spring break, but I need probably $400 to help pay for gas, meals, and a place to stay."

I had just drained my savings account at Citibank, but I still had a line of credit associated with my checking account.

"Do you still have the Citibank card I gave you for emergencies?"

"I think it's somewhere in my purse."

"Take the card, go to Citibank, and withdraw $400. The code is 2019."

"Thanks, Papa. You're the best."

"Are you doing any studying at NYU? How come I never saw your first semester grades?"

"They send all that to Mom with both of your names on the address. And I guess she never forwarded you my grades. Anyway, one A and all the rest B's. I'm giving it my best shot."

"I'm proud of you, Jenny. Can't wait to see you this summer."

"I love you, Papa. I'll send you a postcard from Florida. Hopefully it will make it to your office in Nairobi."

I hung up the phone and had a strange premonition that I wouldn't talk to her again for a long time. I quickly dismissed it and headed down to the Delamere Terrace to meet Nisar.

This time I found him standing next to the bar, and when I began to walk towards him he put down his drink and greeted me with a large smile.

"James, it's so good to see you."

I could already tell that he was assuming that our lunch would be somewhat of a celebration related to my agreeing to work with the investors. I didn't want to let him down immediately, so as a waiter led us to a table, I made pleasant small talk about the phone call to Jenny and the delightful time Melissa and I had dancing under the stars.

Nisar had a small satchel with him, and I wondered if he was expecting me to sign something related to the supposed agreement with the investors.

"I had a wonderful meeting on Tuesday with a few of the lead investors. They will be the big money in this venture, and they are already planning how they will approach the government once the ministry has collapsed."

"That's just it, Nisar. A lot would have to happen for the Bank to pull the funding in the timetable that your friends seem to be envisioning."

"But that's why you and Fortran are involved. You are expediting the process."

"I'm not so sure that David Fortran or I are willing to get that involved in the timing of the Bank's decision."

Nisar stared across the table at me without saying a word. He was stunned by what I had just said. But because of his long history of negotiating deals and compromises, he moved into defense mode and looked directly at me as he spoke.

"Do you know that I have $10,000 for you and $10,000 for Mr. Fortran that I am about to give you as a down payment for your help in this matter?"

I briefly considered the idea of accepting the down payment and not following through, but I knew Nisar would exact a brutal revenge. Better to be completely candid now before I was in too deep.

"That's very generous of the investors, but I can't accept the money."

"And you have spoken to Mr. Fortran, and he is in agreement with this?"

"I know David. He would never accept money to influence a Bank decision."

"So you have spoken to him?"

"I spoke with him on Tuesday morning."

"Do you have nothing else to report?"

"There's a Bank meeting in two weeks to discuss all of the projects in western India. Bombay will undoubtedly be on the agenda."

"You are placing me in an extremely awkward position with the investors. What am I supposed to tell them after you indicated on Monday night that you would help us?"

"I think I said that I would consider the offer."

"You shouldn't have given me that indication, if you were not going to deliver on what we had discussed."

"Saying that I would consider it was not a yes that I was definitely in."

Nisar had not smoked since we had arrived at the table, but now he carefully lit a cigarette and leaned back in his chair.

"If I give you your $10,000, can you promise me that you will attempt to get Fortran on board in the next twenty-four hours?"

"Look Nisar, I told you that I would consider your offer, but nothing more. My guess is that the final decision from the Bank will take months, maybe years. I can't accept money for something I can't deliver."

Nisar just sat there, deeply inhaling his cigarette and staring past me to the lawn that formed the courtyard at The Norfolk.

"Unlike you, James, I do keep my promises, and I have made arrangements for you to meet my associate, Raj Gulati, at the Taj Hotel in Bombay next Wednesday. He will set up the meeting with the judge, and ten days from now, you and your incarcerated friend will be sitting here in Nairobi, enjoying lunch together."

I realized that Nisar was hoping that I would be guilt-stricken by his announcement, and that I would respond in kind by agreeing to talk to David. For a split second, I considered playing that game, as it would give me continued leverage with him and the investors, but the prospect of making a clean break from the whole situation was a much stronger alternative.

"I am deeply indebted to you for making these arrangements. Thank you, Nisar. I am astounded by your generosity. Do I give the money to Raj or to the judge?"

"Raj will be expecting $5,000 for making the connection with the judge. As I mentioned before, the judge will be expecting $25,000 and maybe more."

"What should I do after I meet with the judge?"

"Probably just wait at the Taj. I'm guessing it will take a day or two to get him out."

I felt someone's hand on my shoulder, and from the brightening of Nisar's face I knew it was Melissa. Both of us started to get up, and as Melissa walked around next to me, Nisar extended his right hand.

"I'm delighted to meet you, Mrs. Monroe. My name is Nisar Malik."

"How did you know I was Mrs. Monroe? I could have been one of James's illicit liaisons."

We all laughed and I could see that Nisar couldn't take his eyes off Melissa.

"Your husband and I have become very close. We actually have several things in common, including a penchant for beautiful women."

"You are so right, Mr. Malik. When we first met at Victoria Falls, I had to rescue him from a stunningly attractive woman who already had him in her clutches."

"Why don't you join us for lunch?"

Nisar was clearly anticipating the pleasure of sitting next to Melissa for an hour or two.

"Actually, I've come to tell James that I'm having lunch with Gerard. He has more people for me to meet. I think he knows half of Nairobi."

Nisar was clearly disappointed, but he reverted to his impeccable Indian manners with his goodbyes to Melissa. I thought for a moment that he was going to escort her back to the room. Once she exited, Nisar began to rearrange his satchel and cigarette case as if preparing to leave.

"Aren't we having lunch?"

"Now that your beautiful wife has left, I've lost my motivation to extend our conversation. I will give Raj your number. He should contact you in the next two or three days."

"What will you tell the investors?"

"I'll tell them that I overestimated one man's ability to keep his word."

"That's not really fair."

"Life isn't fair, Mr. Monroe. I'm sure you have learned that by now."

With that, Nisar got up from the table, shook my hand, and gave me a broad smile before exiting the terrace. It was the last time I ever saw him.

CHAPTER SIXTEEN

THE NEXT AFTERNOON, JAMES CALLED THE RCMP OFFICES in Banff to get an update on Charlie. He decided to hold off on calling an attorney until his son was actually arrested. The inspector had handed him a piece of paper with the RCMP number in Banff and Edmonton, and as he pulled the paper out of his wallet, he noticed that the inspector had also written down his cell on the other side.

"Inspector Macpherson."

"Good afternoon, Inspector. James Monroe."

"Mr. Monroe. I was going to call you. Several events have unfolded since we talked yesterday."

"What kind of events?"

"Yesterday afternoon we were able to get into the call history of your daughter's phone, and we located the mechanic she used to work on her car. I actually interviewed him by phone this morning."

"What did he have to say?"

"He acknowledged that he had been up there two or three times to work on her car. The last time he was there—that Friday morning—he claims that he saw your son and daughter arguing in the driveway. At one point he remembered your daughter shouting, "Go to hell!" at your son and then locking him out of the house. Apparently your son stood at the door and yelled obscenities until she finally let him back in."

"I still have a voicemail on my phone that Jenny sent me that morning. There was no mention of any trouble with Charlie. I know Jenny. If there had been an issue she would have mentioned it to me."

"She may not have wanted to upset you."

"What about Charlie's assertion that the mechanic returned that night and that he confronted him in the driveway?"

"I covered that as well. He said his wife would attest to him being home for the entire night."

"Can you tell me the man's name?"

"This is an active investigation and therefore confidential. I've already given you more information than we normally provide—even to family members."

"What happens next?"

"This most recent conversation with the mechanic was, in the short term, the last piece of the puzzle. That, along with the forensic evidence that Charlie has already admitted to, will be enough evidence to take to a judge, and he'll be arrested for the disappearance and possible murder of your daughter. I would highly recommend that you move forward with finding an attorney. After he is formally charged, he'll be moved to the correctional facility in Edmonton."

James ended the call and found the Google application on his phone. He typed in "Attorneys, Banff, Edmonton." He scrolled down. "Henry Moore, Criminal Litigation." He hit the call key on the website and listened as the phone rang twice.

"Henry Moore's office."

"Yes, is Henry Moore there please?"

"Mr. Moore is in court all week, but he normally checks his messages late in the day."

James gave her his contact information, and as soon as the call ended, he saw an incoming call from Vancouver. It was Rob Curtin.

"Hey, J-man, how are things in Lake Louise?"

James loved hearing Rob's friendly voice.

"Things have been better. How's everything there?"

"Full house last night and full house tonight. The laundry room looks like a war zone. Hey, when are you headed back?"

"Hard to say, I'm trying to find an attorney to represent my son. He's gotten himself in somewhat of a scrape. And you probably don't know that my daughter is missing. It's been almost a week."

"Your son called here looking for you last Saturday morning. Never knew you had a son."

"It's a long story, but yes, you were speaking to my son."

James saw that he had an incoming call, so he quickly promised to call Rob back.

"May I please speak to James Monroe?"

"Mr. Moore? Thanks for returning my call so quickly."

"Cheryl just happened to catch me on a break. Tell me what is going on."

"My son, Charlie Benjamin, is about to be arrested for the disappearance and possible murder of my daughter."

"Where is he now?"

"As we speak he's being transferred from an RCMP holding tank in Banff to a correctional facility in Edmonton."

"Have they presented evidence to a judge?"

"They're about to do that."

"Do you have a scanner?"

James had a vague understanding of how you could scan documents on a copier, but he had never used a scanner. Henry Moore could tell that James was clueless, so he didn't wait for a reply.

"How about a fax machine?"

"There's one at the convenience."

"Ok, go to the convenience, get the fax number there, and call my office. Cheryl will fax you a release form that you will need to sign and fax back. That will allow me to talk to Charlie and to be there when they hope to present evidence. Some of what they hope to present could be challenged before it gets to a judge."

"Anything else?"

"Tell me in four or five minutes what happened."

James explained Charlie's unannounced arrival in Lake Louise, the fingerprints on the bathtub, the mechanic in the driveway the next morning, Jenny's disappearance the next afternoon, the truck showing up at 2:00 A.M., and his own arrival in Lake Louise. He ended with Charlie's explanation of the fingerprints on Jenny's robe.

"Any eyewitnesses?"

"The mechanic has been found, and he is claiming that he heard them arguing in the driveway. He said Jenny locked Charlie out of the house."

"Mechanic's name?"

"The inspector wouldn't give me his name."

"Which inspector?"

"His last name is Macpherson."

"Figures. He's nice enough, but then he buries you with the evidence."

"Any other eyewitnesses?"

"Macpherson claims that a neighbor saw Charlie driving Jenny's Saab on Friday afternoon. She probably saw the mechanic."

"What's the name of the neighbor?"

"Not sure. It could have been quite a few people who live fairly close by."

"Is your son married?"

"Yes, he and his wife, Heather, and their son, Ryan, live in Winnetka, Illinois."

"Any domestic violence issues in Charlie's past?"

"None that I know about. But I just met my son a few days ago."

"Do you have his wife's phone number?"

"Nope. I'd have to get it from Charlie."

"How about her email address?"

"Don't have that either."

"Ok, you and Cheryl need to fax back and forth, and I will get her going on finding these names. In the meantime we need to get Heather's phone number."

"Is that it?"

"Unfortunately I'm going to be in court until almost 5:00 P.M. If you want to try another attorney who could get down there this afternoon, I understand. Best I can do is first thing in the morning."

"Thanks, Mr. Moore."

"Sure thing. Oh, by the way, the RCMP is generally very fair, but sometimes they get ahead of themselves, which sounds like what we're seeing here."

James ended the call and thought about calling Rob Curtin back. Despite his normally calm demeanor, his head was spinning. He couldn't begin this process again with a new attorney. Henry Moore seemed competent and aware of every angle. Instead of calling Rob back, he got in his truck and drove to the convenience. He received the fax from Cheryl, signed it, and faxed it back. Henry Moore was now Charlie's best hope of not being arrested, or if the arrest had already occurred, of getting him out on bail.

As he pulled into the driveway, he decided that the best thing he could do for Charlie would be to call Heather. He Googled Charlie's name in Winnetka, and to his surprise, Charlie's name, address, and phone number came right up. He realized that it was almost dinnertime in Chicago, but he figured that would provide a better chance of Heather being home.

"Hello?"

"Is this Heather Benjamin?"

"Speaking."

"Heather, this is James Monroe calling from Alberta, Canada."

"Is Charlie OK?"

James was impressed that her first thought was of Charlie's well-being.

"He's fine, but I think he told you that he is being detained."

"Is he in jail?"

James could hear Ryan in the background asking if his dad was on the phone.

"That's why I'm calling. We're trying to do everything we can to keep him out of jail."

Heather didn't respond, and James could tell that she was desperately trying to hold back the sobs that were welling in the back of her throat.

"Did he do something awful to your daughter?"

"Of course not. Nobody thinks that he did anything to hurt Jenny. But there is some circumstantial evidence that they are trying to use against him."

"Do you mean being alone with your daughter?"

"Yes, that and a few other things. We may get to the point where they will want to talk to you, so I just want you to be prepared in case they call or Charlie's attorney calls."

"Charlie has an attorney in Canada?"

"I just found an attorney for him a few hours ago, so he may call you."

"What would he ask me?"

"He just wants to be sure that Charlie has not had any domestic violence issues in the past."

Heather didn't respond for about ten seconds. James's heart began to drop. "This will be the death knell," he thought.

"We've had one domestic violence issue that happened about four years ago, before Charlie's dad got sick. We were cooking out and planning to have dinner in the backyard. Richard and Charlie were arguing about some investment that Charlie had made. He needed a cosigner, and Richard had reluctantly signed. The deal went belly-up. Of course Richard didn't want to assume any of the liability, and Charlie kept screaming at him over and over 'Then why did you sign?' The whole thing escalated, and Ryan and I rushed out of the kitchen to try to quiet them down.

"Ryan got between them just as Charlie shoved his dad. Richard fell backwards and Ryan just happened to be behind him as he fell. Ryan started screaming, 'He broke my arm; he broke my arm.' Instead of stopping, Charlie screamed at his dad, 'Get up faker, you're not hurt.' Ryan thought that Charlie was screaming at him. He went into a high-pitched wail that sounded like a trapped animal. The neighbors called the police and two squad cars arrived in about five minutes.

"No one was charged, but a report was filed with the Winnetka police, and Charlie later received a letter saying the report would remain on file until 2027. Charlie hired an attorney to try to get the report removed, but he couldn't do a thing."

James didn't respond for almost a minute, just allowing the potential impact of Heather's story to line up with the evidence already there. He knew that a prosecuting attorney would jump on "previous offenses" and "anger management issues" to put Charlie away for at least thirty years, maybe for life. Plus the mechanic's story of Jenny and Charlie arguing before her disappearance would dovetail perfectly with the domestic violence report already on file. It was the perfect storm of incriminating evidence, but somehow, for Heather, he needed to remain upbeat.

"That's very helpful Heather. I know that not having Charlie there must be very difficult."

Heather's throat tightened as she fought back tears. She could barely speak.

"When you see Charlie, tell him that Ryan and I miss him and we love him very much."

She was barely able to get the words out, but now it was James who was almost speechless.

"Have a good evening, Heather. You're a good wife and a good mom. We will get through this. Charlie needs our love and support, and of course he also needs our prayers."

James put down the phone, found Charlie's suitcase, and began to pack clothes and personal belongings that they might allow him to have in prison. He decided to drive to Edmonton first thing in the morning to hopefully see Charlie and meet Henry Moore.

Now that he knew about the domestic violence report that was permanently on file in Winnetka, his options were narrowing to only one possibility. He had to find his daughter, and in doing so, also save his son.

CHAPTER SEVENTEEN

RAJ GULATI PHONED ME AT THE NORFOLK TWO DAYS later to say that he had arranged a meeting at the Taj Mahal hotel in Bombay for Wednesday afternoon. The judge had requested that no names be used, but Raj had given him Jonathan's name so that he could explore the particulars of the case.

I was to meet Raj in my hotel room at 3:30 P.M., and the meeting with the judge would be thirty minutes later. He requested his $5,000 to be in American money, and he told me that the judge had upped his fee from $25,000 to $30,000. I had already done a wire transfer of $25,000 from Citibank in New York, so the next day, I arranged a $10,000 loan from my retirement account with the World Bank. Melissa had been effusive in her gratitude for what I was doing and promised to pay me back within a year. Still, I had given her the wrong impression regarding my personal wealth, and she assumed that in the grand scheme of things $25,000 or $35,000 was probably just money I would have spent on a second car. Essentially she believed that I would not miss it. I had paid for everything since we had left Victoria Falls, so she had begun to assume my largesse in all financial dealings.

When I made my airplane and hotel reservations the next day, I was tempted to put it on my corporate card with the Bank, but that would have been a deception, so I used a personal card to reserve the plane and the room. Since I was carrying "financial instruments" in excess of $10,000, I would have to use my World Bank credentials to get $35,000 in cash through customs in Bombay. It would not be difficult since World Bank officials sometimes were required to handle large sums of currency. It occurred to me that Melissa would have had a great deal of difficulty bringing that much cash into India.

On the morning of my departure, I packed the cash into a case that had a World Bank insignia on the side, and I made Xerox copies of my Bank credentials. Since I only anticipated being in Bombay for a few days—certainly no longer than a week—I packed a small suitcase and grabbed a cab to Jomo Kenyatta airport in Nairobi. With my World Bank credentials, I breezed through customs and caught the 6:00 A.M. flight to Bombay. It was a six-hour flight, but because of the two-hour time difference, it was 2:00 P.M. local time when I arrived at the Bombay airport.

After seeing my World Bank credentials, the only questions I received from the customs official were to find out where I was staying and my expected return date. He even seemed unconcerned when I told him that my return date was uncertain. The big surprise was that he didn't ask me to open the $35,000 case. I had reported the cash on my customs form and apparently that was enough.

As I walked out of the airport and headed for the taxi stand, the first thing I noticed was the heat and humidity. April and May are the end of summer in Kenya, but May in Bombay is one of the hottest months to be followed in July by the beginning of the monsoon. The airport is only about twenty miles north of the center of the city, but depending on the time of day, the trip can take over an hour.

As you get closer to the city center, the mass of humanity inhabiting the heart of Bombay becomes more intense, and the vibrancy of the city begins to throb in your ears even within the cocoon of a closed car. It has always amazed me how millions of people can inhabit such a small space, and yet somehow Bombay thrives in spite of itself. Its moniker is "Gateway to India," and as the major port city on the west coast, it seems to embrace all of the best (and the worst) of Indian culture.

It is a mishmash of religions, architecture, socio-economic groups, and artistic expression. It has incredibly wealthy enclaves—such as the Taj Hotel—and slums that would rival the worst of any South American city. There are street gangs and drugs and a subculture of black market goods ranging from prostitution to electronics. The best and the worst of humanity are here, and if you are wise as an outsider, you remain intentional about the purpose of your visit and keep aware of what is going on around you.

Raj Gulati knocked on the door of my hotel room exactly at 3:30. He was wearing a business suit, and despite the heat, he had on a tie. From the moment he walked in, he seemed preoccupied and somewhat uncomfortable with my questions.

"Should I discuss Jonathan Samuel's case with the judge or just give him the money?"

"He will probably ask you a few questions. It's hard to say."

"How do you know Nisar Malik? Is he a business partner?"

"I'd rather not talk about Nisar. I agreed to set up this meeting, and for me that's where this ends."

"How do you know the judge will show up? Or to put it another way, what do I do if he doesn't show up?"

"Here's my card. If he doesn't show up, contact me, and I'll return the money."

Although the meeting with Raj was beginning to feel one-sided, what choice did I have? If I didn't give him the $5,000, he could easily call the judge and cancel the meeting. I would return to Nairobi to tell Melissa that the whole thing had fallen through.

I opened the case, counted out $5,000, and handed it to Raj. He took the money, gave me a quick bow, and exited. He seemed amateurish compared to Nisar, but if he set up the meeting, he had done his job. I sat on the bed and looked at my watch. I still had fifteen minutes before the judge arrived, and I thought back to the day I had first met Melissa at the Devil's Pool. I remembered feeling inadequate as I stood on the bank witnessing her rescue. I was the spectator. The real action was in the current itself, with Melissa swimming for her life and the man of courage pulling her to safety.

Now I had become that man. I was in Bombay on a rescue operation to save her brother, and Melissa was on the sidelines, helpless to do much more than to cheer me on. I heard the knock at the door. I quickly moved the case off to the side, walked across the room, and pulled open the door. To my surprise, there was not one man, but three men, although the man in the middle was clearly the judge.

"May I come in?"

As they entered, I offered all three men a chair. The judge sat down directly across from me, and after lighting a cigarette, and looking briefly around the room, he looked directly at me.

"Tell me why I'm here today."

It was not the question I was expecting, although I hadn't considered how the conversation might begin.

"Didn't Mr. Gulati tell you the purpose of the meeting?"

"He told me that you had come to Bombay on behalf of your friend whose brother is awaiting trial for smuggling drugs. I've looked into the case and there's very little I am able to do."

My mind was racing. Was this the preamble that every corrupt judge used before accepting a bribe, or did he honestly not know the purpose of the meeting? What had Raj told him, or more importantly, what instructions had Nisar given to Raj? I decided that ambiguity would be the safest course.

"Raj made me aware that you might be in a position to help Jonathan Samuel, but apparently that may not be the case."

"Are you offering me a bribe?"

If I said no, then I had come to Bombay for nothing. If I said yes, then either Jonathan would be freed and we would fly back together to Nairobi, or it was entrapment, and I would be arrested on the spot for a capital offense.

"I am asking that you accept $30,000 US for helping Jonathan Samuel to be set free."

"Do you have the money here? May I see it?"

I walked across the room and grabbed the case. All three men leaned forward in their chairs as I undid the latches.

The judge glanced at the money and then with one finger directed the man to his left toward the bedside telephone. A part of me assumed that the judge was directing the man to call the prison to procure Jonathan's release. But wouldn't the judge make that call himself? It was at that moment that the man on the right removed a small tape recorder from his breast pocket and clicked it off. I had just been trapped into offering an Indian judge a bribe.

I could hear the man on the phone speaking very softly in Hindi. The only thing I recognized was my room number, which he repeated several times. The judge pulled out a cigarette, lit it, and again looked directly at me.

"Did your friend Raj not tell you that I am known in my court for disliking Americans and arrogant Brits?"

I couldn't even speak, so I just nodded my head. Nisar must have instructed Raj to arrange a meeting with one of the toughest judges in Bombay, and I had walked into the setup.

"Did you know that my sister went to college for two years in the United States?"

He didn't wait for my reply.

"She was not treated well in the dormitory where she lived. In fact, she was harassed to the point that she finally returned home."

"I'm sorry that happened. Not all students from India are treated that way."

"And now your friend screws up, and you think all that is required is to bribe a judge with $30,000 and all will be forgotten?"

"I was trying to help a friend."

"How about the poor people from the state of Maharashtra who became addicted to the drugs that your friend smuggled into Bombay? Are they left to suffer while your friend is released?"

"I'm sorry about the drugs."

Suddenly I didn't know what I was saying. I wanted to sound sympathetic, but my responses were coming off as insincere.

"There are a few judges in Maharashtra who might take a bribe, but instead I will take your money and distribute it in the neighborhoods that have been ravaged by illegal narcotics."

I couldn't imagine him actually doing that, but as he said it he pulled the case onto his lap and carefully snapped it shut.

"We'll think of it as America's contribution to Bombay's war on crime."

He now got up, took the case, and headed for the bathroom. I heard the door latch and the man who had the tape recorder and I were left alone. The man who had made the calls was standing guard in front of the door.

"Do you know how screwed you are?"

I was surprised that he had said anything to me.

"They are going to take you directly to Arthur Road Jail and lock you up. Look, do you have any other cash?"

For a moment I thought he was going to ask for any other money I might still have so that he could take it, but instead he began to whisper.

"When the judge comes out, ask to use the bathroom. He may want me to go in there with you. Either way, take the largest bills you have, roll them up and stick them up your rear as far as they will go. Believe me, where you are going, the only language of reprieve will be cash."

The judge was making his way out of the bathroom, and he was still holding onto the case. He came back over and sat down.

"May I use the bathroom?"

"Sure, but Amar will go with you."

Amar and I both got up and headed to the bathroom. I had three one-hundred dollar bills in my wallet and some small bills that probably totaled another hundred.

As he closed the door and bolted us in, I'm sure he could see that I was shaking.

"Roll up the three hundreds as tight as they will go, and stick them up there. You'll know they are safe when they are pulled up in the opposite direction."

With both of my hands shaking so much that I could barely handle the money, I rolled up the bills and inserted them as far as they would go. I felt ashamed and violated as I fumbled with each bill. Instead of turning away, Amar continued to watch the entire process. After several tries I could feel them get pulled deeper inside.

"Do you have a pen?"

He pulled out a pen from the same pocket where he had hidden the recorder. I took the rest of the money out of my wallet and handed it to him.

"I want you to make three phone calls for me. The first one will be to my daughter's dormitory at NYU. She won't be there until next week, but you need to speak directly to her."

I scribbled the number on the back of one of my business cards and wrote "Jenny Monroe" next to it.

"Tell her that I am on special mission for the World Bank, and I don't know when I will be able to contact her. Tell her that I said not to worry."

I still had a receipt from The Norfolk, and on the receipt was the phone number of the hotel.

"Call this number in Nairobi. Ask for Mrs. Monroe in Room 17. Tell her that I've been arrested and I need her help. If you know where I am going to jail, give her that information as well. Finally, call this third number in America. Ask for Teresa Benjamin and tell her all that you know about my arrest."

Amar stuffed the cards, the receipt and the cash into his side pocket and then shook my hand.

We could hear men's voices on the other side of the door, and as Amar undid the latch I could see the judge talking to all four of them. They were big. Two of them had beards, and they looked more like street thugs than police officers. The judge handed them something—I guessed it was money from the case—and gave them instructions in Hindi.

One of the men walked towards me, pulling out handcuffs from a black bag that hung from his belt. After quickly frisking me, he held my two hands in front of me and snapped on the cuffs. The cuff on my left wrist was already pinching the bone just above my hand. Once the cuffs were on, the judge walked over to me, and I thought for a moment that he was about to hit me.

"I told them that you like to help drug dealers who come to Bombay to make a profit off the backs of the Indian people. Shame on you. You are not part of the solution, you are part of the problem."

He picked up the case and headed for the door.

"By the way, Mr. Monroe, for the fifteen flights down to the lobby, I told these men that you preferred to take the stairs."

It was the only time that he had addressed me by my name, and it confirmed that I had not been part of some bizarre mistake. Nisar had instructed Raj to contact one of the cruelest judges in Bombay, and he had just walked out the door with the money I had carefully saved for Jenny's second year at NYU.

Until we got out into the hallway and headed towards the stairwell, I had no idea what the judge meant when he said I preferred the stairs. Once we got into the stairwell, the men instructed me to sit on the top stair, and the two men who were now below me each grabbed an ankle. Before I had time to consider what might be next, the two men with my ankles began to pull me down the stairs.

Without the use of my hands, I had no way to cushion each successive fall. And the concrete edge of each stair dug into my lower back. It was everything I could do to keep my head leaning forward so that the stairs did not slam into the back of my skull, but the two men walking down behind me would occasionally put their shoe on my forehead so that I could not lean forward.

They were talking and laughing in Hindi, and at one point, after four or five flights, they asked me in English if I wanted to reconsider the elevator. When I didn't reply one of them said, "Show him the elevator!" And with that the four of them lifted me over the railing, threatening to drop me into the vacuum of space that extended down for another eleven floors.

Two of them grabbed the chain on my handcuffs so that I was swinging back and forth, fully extended above the abyss, held only by the cuffs. The pain in my wrists and the lower part of my hands was excruciating. At one point they stopped and pulled me back over the railing until one of them screamed "Not your floor?" With hysterical laughter they swung me back over and repeated "the elevator" several times.

Finally they resumed pulling me down the stairs and I could feel the vertebrae being smashed in my lower back. I had bruises all up and down my back and legs and the back of my head was bleeding.

When we reached the lobby level of the stairway, I tried to get up, but there was a sharp pain in the upper part of my legs and lower back that convinced me I was partially paralyzed. The men unclasped the cuffs, draped my arms over their shoulders, and led me out to a waiting car. A few people looked up, but for all they knew, I was drunk and being assisted by friends.

Two of the men sat in the front of the car and I was placed in the middle of the back seat, flanked by the other two. Because of the damage to my lower back and the small space I was given, I couldn't get comfortable. I discovered that moving forward a little on the seat provided some relief, but the man on the passenger side of the front seat warned me once to sit back. I did move back a few inches, but that was apparently not enough. He suddenly came over the seat and landed two ferocious punches to my nose and eye so that now there was blood all over my face and down the front of my shirt. For a moment I thought I would pass out from the pain, but even in that delirium I could still hear him shouting, "Do you want another one? I said, sit back!" The men to my left and right seemed oblivious to the blood, which was now covering part of the seat, and because of the handcuffs, I was only able to wipe some of it from my nose and eye.

After about thirty minutes we arrived at what appeared to be a police station, and I was ceremoniously carried inside into a small anteroom. The same man who hit me in the face presented the officer on duty with a letter—presumably from the judge—and then came in and sat next to me, never offering any assistance with the blood that had started to coagulate around my left eye.

With my right eye, I could see that I was at a station in a part of Bombay known as Kanjurmarg, and for almost thirty minutes I stared at a commendation that had been awarded to the Kanjurmarg Police in 1988 for lowering the crime rate from the two previous years. The chief of police was in the picture along with a judge. It was impossible to determine if the judge in the photo was my judge from earlier that day.

Finally, the officer in charge appeared, and the man who hit me helped him get me into a cell. The two of them flanked me—I still could not walk—and dragged me through two heavily barred security barriers to a small cell that had a toilet and a cot, but no sink. There was a blanket on the cot, but it looked like it had not been cleaned in well over a year. As the two of them clanged the cell door behind them, the officer had a slight grin, as if he was about to say something. Instead, my thug friend gave me a parting thought for the evening.

"Enjoy Kanjurmarg. This place is paradise compared to Arthur Road, and you'll be there soon enough."

I had heard about Arthur Road Jail. It had the reputation of being the worst hellhole prison in India and one of the worst prisons in the world. If that was where I was headed, maybe I was lucky to spend my first night alone. I knelt down next to the toilet and removed my shirt. The front of it was covered with blood, but the back had a few places that had not been torn apart by the ride down the stairs. There was a little bit of water in the bottom of the toilet, and I carefully dipped my shirt into the water and began to dab away the dried blood on my face and the back of my head.

There was no mirror, but after wiping away as much blood as I could, I used the shirt as a compress to put on my eye that had swollen shut. My nose was broken and though the bleeding had stopped, there was still blood coagulated in my nostrils; the makeshift compress provided some relief to my nose as well.

I crawled over to the cot, and lying on my side, I was able to wedge part of the blanket up against the wall to provide some support for my back. I hadn't eaten since having a sandwich on the plane, and I was tired and maimed from the stairs. As I began a restless night, I thought of Melissa, probably dancing on the Delamere Terrace with Gerard Hugel. At least I had managed to have Amar get a message to her, and with all of her ingenuity and resourcefulness she would undoubtedly find a way to get me out of Bombay and back to Nairobi. Since all of this had been done for her, it was her turn to reciprocate, and I had to believe that she would respond with the same kindness and generosity that I had shown her since the day we first met.

I was awakened the next morning by the sharp clang of prison doors, and a young man (probably not more than twenty) appeared in my cell with a small plate of poha and some coffee. He also had a small cup, and in the cup were three ice cubes. I thanked him profusely and managed to find out that his name was Sunil. I wasn't sure if the ice cubes were his idea or not, but I immediately wrapped two of the cubes in my shirt and applied the compress to my left eye, which was now completely swollen shut. I touched around my nose and it felt bulbous as if it were now twice its original size. The blows to the back of my head had resulted in a raging headache that kept me awake for part of the night, so I pressed the third cube into the base of my skull.

That little bit of relief to my face and my neck allowed me to sit up and sip coffee, and I used my fingers to sample the poha. It was the first food I'd eaten since lunch the day before, and although it was bland, I ate every grain of rice. The coffee helped my head to clear, and to my surprise, my back felt somewhat better. About an hour later, the same officer who had walked me to my cell the night before appeared with a clipboard, and instead of sitting, he leaned up against the wall next to the cot and began to ask me questions.

He seemed surprised that I had arrived at the Kanjurmarg station without identification, and I told him several times that my passport, my World Bank credentials, and my return plane ticket were all in my room at the Taj Hotel. When I mentioned the World Bank, he continued to fill out another form on his clipboard and then paused without looking directly at me.

"Is the World Bank aware that one of its own is a drug smuggler?"

Apparently the judge had told his squadron of thugs that I had smuggled drugs as further motivation for them to teach me a lesson on the way to Kanjurmarg. I thought about protesting the officer's assessment of me as a drug smuggler—actually, I had only attempted to bribe a judge—but I saw the futility in arguing over why I was there. If he was completing a report to have me incarcerated at Arthur Road Jail, I wasn't sure which felony would be regarded there with more derision.

Essentially I was being "booked," and the officer was more concerned with filling every blank on the form than he was with the particulars of my crime. He also didn't say a word about my swollen face or the way that I was haphazardly sprawled across the cot to find the most comfortable position for my back.

When he finished filling out five or six forms, he must have read in the instructions, "Finally, ask the prisoner if he or she has any questions." He read it to me verbatim.

"Do I have the right to contact an attorney?"

"Of course. If you give me the name and number, I will make the call for you."

"May I see a telephone book?"

"We don't provide phone books for prisoner use."

"Then how am I supposed to find an attorney?"

"This is not really my problem. However, if you don't have your own attorney, the state of Maharashtra will provide an attorney for you."

"Don't you see that it would be easier to simply give me a Bombay directory?"

"I have already told you that we do not provide telephone books to prisoners, but I am happy to make the call if you have a name and number for me."

I remembered from working with Indian officials on World Bank projects that the rules of protocol in India were sometimes byzantine. It was all about the letter of the law, no matter how unreasonable or draconian those rules and laws might be. He wasn't going to budge on the phone book issue.

"Ok, then I would like to request an attorney from the state."

"You have to be incarcerated for at least two weeks to request an attorney from the state of Maharashtra."

I lay back on my cot and looked at the ceiling. Not only was I headed to the worst prison in western India, but I was also dealing with the most uncooperative government regulations known to man.

"So then, are there any more additional questions?"

"No, I have no more questions."

I could see that he had checked off his final box on the form, so from his perspective, the interview was over. He started to pull back the iron bar that secured the entrance to the cell, and then he paused.

"By the way, we'll be moving you in the morning to Arthur Road, so you may want to request a shower down the hall sometime this evening. It may be the last time for months that you will actually feel clean."

After he left, I was encouraged that I could actually stand up and hobble around the cell. I was hoping that my vertebrae had been severely bruised but not broken. There was some paralysis in my right leg, but I hoped that would also improve as the swelling in my back began to decrease. That evening I took a shower and allowed the warm spray to move back and forth across the back of my neck. If I hadn't had this brief reprieve at Kanjurmarg I could have easily died before my arrival at Arthur Road. I was still banged up, but my current discomfort was only a fraction of what I was to experience over the next nine months.

The next morning, I was led out to a Kanjurmarg police van and delivered to Arthur Road Jail. When the doors of the van opened, I was surprised to see a crowd of people, and for a moment I thought that the word was out that a World Bank official had been arrested for bribing a judge—or, even worse, smuggling drugs. I was later to find that many of the people standing on the outside of the prison were there to deliver contraband to inmates who either had the cash or the connections to beat the system.

I was led through the crowds to the main doorway, and because of my swollen nose and eye, people probably assumed I was part of a gang war and had been arrested the night before for gang violence. They brought me to what appeared to be a cashier's window, and the same Kanjurmarg officer who had interviewed me the day before handed the man behind the small bars my paperwork.

"No passport?"

"All of my identification is at the Taj Hotel."

The man behind the bars sneered.

"You'll find the accommodations here very similar to the Taj Mahal."

Both men laughed and the man behind the screen repeated "Taj Mahal" several times as he rifled through my paperwork. He then said something to the Kanjurmarg officer in Hindi, and the man quickly exited. The man behind the screen pushed a buzzer located on the desk next to him, and a large bearded man appeared who looked remarkably identical to one of the thugs who had subjected me to the abuse in the stairwell. He led me out of the cubicle and into a large room where there were twenty-five or thirty men sitting naked on the floor. The room smelled of human sweat and urine, and I noticed a corner of the room where the naked men had gone to urinate or defecate.

"Take off your clothes and put them in this basket."

I quickly realized that I was expected to undress right there, and the man watched me intently as I removed all of my clothing. I put everything in the basket and handed it to him.

"Wait until your name is called."

I walked over to what appeared to be the end of the line, and sat down on the cold concrete floor. The man just ahead of me had his face buried in his crossed arms, and I couldn't tell if he was sleeping or just tuning out the world around him.

"How long have you been waiting?"

I said it loudly enough that I was sure he heard me. He didn't respond.

"How long have you been waiting in line?"

He didn't verbally respond, but held up two fingers.

"Two hours?"

The man shook his head back and forth.

"Two days?"

I was actually kidding when I said it, so I was shocked when he nodded his head in the affirmative.

"How about these other men? How long have they waited?"

He held up five fingers.

"They have been waiting for five days?"

He nodded his head.

"Do they feed you?"

I had been interviewing the man as if I were a journalist, and now I suddenly realized that my plight was identical to every naked man in the room.

"They feed us one bowl of dal a day, but it is disgusting and filled with dirty water."

"Where do we sleep?"

"They give each of us one blanket for the night. You will not want to use it. It is filled with lice."

"How many men do they process from this room each day?"

"Usually four or five, but yesterday it was nine. There was a man here yesterday who had been here for at least four days. He died last night, and they removed his body early this morning. They probably want us to die here to give them more space in the barracks."

I thought about the $300 that was still stuffed up my rectum. I guessed that when someone was called out of this holding tank they were probably examined, and I didn't want to risk having to defecate and then reinsert the money while the entire room was watching. I decided that I would keep myself hydrated—maybe even drink the watery dal, but I had to avoid defecating until I was officially processed. I was beginning to believe what Amar had said about money being the only source of reprieve at Arthur Road.

As it turned out, I was processed after only two days in the holding tank, and as I was led away by a guard, I felt bad for those who had been waiting twice that long. I was examined by a man who had a white mask over his face, and he wore surgical gloves. He thoroughly examined my rectum, but he didn't go high enough to discover any bills. While I was in the holding tank I had spoken to a man who was being processed at Arthur Road for the third time in the past six years. He explained that because of the over-crowding—three thousand men and women in a jail designed to accommodate eight hundred—the jail essentially deputized some of the long-term inmates, and they were the ones who had more direct contact with prisoners. Some of them were even referred to as wardens, and if anyone was to be bribed, it would be the wardens, not the guards. The guards had a supervisory role, but they rarely got into confrontations with inmates.

After the physical examination, I was told that I could find my clothes at the end of a long hallway that connected the infirmary to the barracks. I entered the hallway still completely naked, and to my surprise, there were about twenty men—I surmised that they were the wardens—who were waiting for my exit from the infirmary. I wasn't sure how they were alerted to be ready for new prisoners who were looking for their clothes, but at the sight of me they formed two lines—a gauntlet—and they each had a bamboo stick that was flayed at the end to slice into the skin. One of the men near the head of the gauntlet had a whistle, and he stepped out of the line and walked towards me.

"Are you looking for your clothes?"

He didn't wait for my reply.

"These men and I are here to help you find them! When you hear the whistle blow once, you should head down the hallway. A double whistle means you must come back and start over.Are you English?"

"No, American."

"Even better. Now wait for the whistle."

He blew the whistle and I headed into the gauntlet. I was hoping that my swollen eye and nose would cause them to go easy on me, but instead it seemed to have the opposite effect. I was to find out that perceived weakness in prison is an invitation for more abuse. The men were screaming in Hindi and thrashing every part of my body with the flayed bamboo. Each strike produced a small cut on my skin, so that as I reached the end of the gauntlet, I was already covered in blood. I was almost to the last man, and I could see baskets of clothes stacked up at the end of the hallway.

The men were screaming for the double whistle, and just as I passed the last man, I heard its shrill double report echo down the hallway. I turned around, thinking that they would allow me to walk back to the beginning, but the idea was for me to fight my way back to the start through an intensified barrage of bamboo. Every strike was becoming excruciatingly painful, and at one point I stumbled and fell to the floor.

"Get up, English! Get up and be a man!"

The din of their taunts subsided a little when I reached the place where I had started, but I had barely arrived there when I heard the whistle blow again. I headed back down the gauntlet covering my face as best I could, but when I arrived at the end, the flays of bamboo had reopened the wounds on my eye and nose.

I could barely see the baskets because of the blood on my eyes and face, but I finally found the clothes I had on when I arrived at Arthur Road. I was led into the barracks and directed to a large room that had one sink and one toilet for the sixty men who were packed like sardines into a twenty-by-forty-foot space. There was one window at the top of one wall, and it was reinforced by iron bars. Most of the men tried to sit or lie as far away as possible from the sink and toilet.

With sixty men trying to use one toilet, it had constantly overflowed so that there was urine and feces in a three-foot perimeter around the flooded facility. New prisoners were assigned to the toilet end of the room, and so when a few inmates scooted over to make a small space for me, I was only ten feet away from the filth and the stench.

I forced myself to take off my shirt, and I waded through the putrid slime to get to the sink. I drenched part of my shirt with water and went back to my spot to carefully dab away the blood from my fresh wounds. Others looked at me knowingly, since undoubtedly they had also been subjected to the gauntlet, but no one offered to help me in any way. This was a room where most had lost all sense of their humanity, and they had become incapable of care for others or even themselves.

As I look back on my months at Arthur Road, I am grateful that I was able to use my $300 to extricate myself from the harshest realities of the prison during the first three months I was there. Because I had some money, I was able to buy my way into less offensive living conditions, and the people I lived with from May to July were gang members and drug smugglers who maintained their slightly better accommodations through cash that was smuggled in from the outside.

A favorite ploy of theirs was to have one of their people on the outside show up at a prisoner's court appearance. They would pay him to bring money back into Arthur Road, and their lifestyle was maintained. Because the word had gotten around that I was in for smuggling drugs, I was often approached by gang members who either wanted drugs or wanted my advice on how to smuggle drugs into Bombay. My reputation as a drug smuggler actually gave me a certain prestige that I worked hard to maintain for about half of my time in prison.

By August, I was completely out of money, and the wardens who I had been paying off during the first several months were becoming impatient with me continuing to enjoy better living conditions.

In early September, I was moved back into a room very similar to the room I had been assigned immediately after the gauntlet, and that is when my health and my spirits began to rapidly decline.

Like the earlier room, there was filth and stench everywhere. Many of the inmates had skin disease, and at night the lights were left on. Inmates were constantly getting up and making their way to the toilet, and there were men who mumbled incoherently all day and night. I still think of it as an antechamber of hell. I used to close my eyes when I was there and think of being on the train with Melissa or the night we had danced together in Nairobi. This was all short-lived, as it was inevitably interrupted by someone screaming or another person bumping into me on the way to the toilet. Because of the putrid conditions, I began to develop a cough and my own saliva began to taste like the room and the stench of urine.

It was in late September when I first met Ramesh. He was young and probably only twenty years old. He had been accused of murdering his uncle, and like most of the inmates of Arthur Road, he was there awaiting trial. For some reason, the wardens didn't like him (Ramesh attributed their dislike to his laughter the first time through the gauntlet) and they would sometimes pull him out of the room at night and beat him for their own amusement. One night they raped him, and he returned wounded and ashamed. I could hear his whimpering until almost dawn the next day.

Despite all of this, Ramesh maintained a fairly positive attitude, and he always wore his New York Yankees ball cap. He dreamed of going to New York City one day, and he knew most of the Yankee players and even their batting averages. He liked that I had a connection with New York, and he was fascinated by Jenny being at NYU.

For over four months, I had been promised a state attorney, and finally at the end of September, I was notified that we had an appointment the next day. I was led into an area where there were several prisoners sitting across the table from visitors. The meeting was set for 1:00 P.M., and I waited patiently for his or her arrival.

At about 1:10, a Catholic nun came into the room and sat across from me.

"Are you Ashmit?"

"Actually my name is James."

"I didn't think you looked Indian. I have an appointment to meet with Ashmit, but he may have not received the message."

"And I am supposed to meet an attorney provided by the state, but apparently they aren't coming."

"Are you an American?"

"I live in New York."

"How did you end up here?"

I noticed that she was fairly young, probably in her late twenties, and her complexion was flawless. Mostly I noticed the brightness of her eyes.

As I told her my story from the time I met Melissa at Victoria Falls to my arrest at the Taj Mahal, she seemed truly interested. I told the entire narrative in about five minutes, and when I ended there was an awkward silence.

"Have you ever thought that all of the events of your life have led to this moment?"

"I'm not sure what you mean."

"What I suppose I mean is this may be your time."

"How is it my time?"

"This may be the moment in your life where God finally has you where he wants you! So make the most of it."

"And do what?"

"Show him that you are capable of helping other people, of caring for them."

Her eyes were glistening as she said the part about caring for other people, and there was a resonance in the way she said it that almost made me feel I was talking directly to God.

As if on cue, my state attorney entered the room and the guard directed him over to me.She noticed that someone was now standing behind her, and she smiled as she got up from her chair. As she turned to leave, she looked directly at me.

"Become that person, James. Take your baby steps, but become the person you have always secretly hoped you would be."

I watched her flowing habit as she exited the vestibule of the prison. Perhaps it wasn't by chance that my attorney was late and Ashmit didn't show. Perhaps our five-minute meeting was something planned from the day I was born. I didn't hear a word that the state attorney said for the first ten minutes of our meeting. All I could think about was "This may be your time."

That evening I lay sleeping only a few feet away from Ramesh. Despite the adverse sleeping conditions, he was sleeping soundly, but since it was Friday I knew that the wardens might come in the middle of the night to pull him out and beat him.

About an hour later, I carefully removed Ramesh's Yankees hat and placed it on my own head. Since we were about the same height and weight, I didn't think they would notice the switch when they came to get him.

It was late, probably 3:00 A.M., when I felt a boot dig into the side of my abdomen. Three men were standing over me chatting in Hindi, and one of them yanked my arm so hard that I thought it had come out of its socket. They blindfolded me and dragged me out of the room and down a long corridor to a room without windows. I could see a little through the blindfold, enough to see that one of the men was the warden with the whistle when I had been forced to run the gauntlet. He was the one who ordered the other two men to strip off my clothes so that I was then naked and blindfolded and standing in the middle of the room. All three men had been drinking, and they continued to pass a bottle back and forth as they took a large rope and wrapped it around me from my ankles to my neck.

I had heard of "the helicopter" from other inmates who had been pulled from the barracks in the middle of the night, but even with their specific accounts, I had never understood the logistics of this particular humiliation.

There was a large meat hook suspended from the ceiling, and the hook was able to pivot in a 360-degree rotation. The three men lifted me up and fastened the meat hook with a clip to the rope, so that I was now horizontally suspended from the ceiling with only my head and feet free from the rope's restraint. Because of the angle of the rope, my head was facing the ceiling along with my toes. While I hung there with my back to the floor, one of the men took his lit cigarette and put it out on the middle of my left foot.

Before they began to spin me, I could see that each of them had a bamboo cane with the end flayed—the same bamboo I had experienced in the gauntlet, only now my neck and face were completely unprotected.

The men positioned themselves at equal points below my circumference, and they began to spin me much as small children spin a merry-go-round. Because I was facing the ceiling and my arms were tied down, I had no way to establish any equilibrium, and this produced a loss of groundedness that I can only describe as the feeling you sometimes experience on an airplane in turbulent weather when the plane hits air pockets and any sense of gravity evaporates. The faster they spun me, the worse that feeling became, and I soon began to vomit. Because of the speed of my circumference, it was only with a great deal of difficulty that I was able to slightly turn my head and avoid drowning. My throat was partially blocked with vomit; I was dizzy and it became nearly impossible to breathe through my nose.

Finally the spinning slowed down and stopped. The men sat down on cement blocks and continued to drink and smoke cigarettes. They asked me several questions in Hindi, and I could only attribute their inability to distinguish me from Ramesh to their drunken state. I guessed that they had been drinking since much earlier that evening, and ironically their heavy drinking probably saved me from being raped.

After about ten minutes, they started to spin me in the other direction, only this time as I whizzed past them, they made a game of cracking me across the neck with the bamboo and spitting on my face so that my nostrils began to fill with both vomit and saliva. They gave my feet a similar whacking with the bamboo, so that when they finally took me down, my feet were cut and bleeding and my neck and face were covered in saliva and blood.

Somehow I managed to remember Ramesh's hat as they pulled me back down the corridor and into my barracks. As I lay there dabbing away the blood, I looked over at Ramesh. He was still sleeping soundly, and as I carefully placed his Yankee's hat back on his head I began to get a glimpse of the care for others that the nun had mentioned earlier.

Before I drifted off into a state of semi-consciousness, I felt an elation in my heart that I had never known before. Up until that moment, I had believed that the most exquisite joy to be found in this world was in the arms of a woman. Now, for the first time in my life, I knew that the highest good was personal sacrifice for others so that my friend did not have to go through another night of torture.

CHAPTER EIGHTEEN

EARLY THE NEXT MORNING, JAMES DROVE THE FOUR hours from Lake Louise to Edmonton. He had some of Charlie's clothes and personal items, as well as a letter that he had written to his son the night before. Before leaving, he had called Henry Moore's office and spoken to Cheryl. There was really no reason for Henry Moore to drive to Edmonton. Macpherson had succeeded in bringing the evidence before a judge the previous afternoon, and so Charlie was officially under arrest. There was no information as yet regarding a court hearing, but Cheryl thought it would probably be in the next ten days.

When James arrived at the Edmonton Correctional Facility, he was immediately impressed by its newness and its cleanliness. His own prison experience in India had been the exact opposite. But he knew that Charlie was nevertheless reeling from the arrest and his transport to an actual correctional facility.

A uniformed woman in the reception area had James fill out visitation forms, and then she guided him down a labyrinth of hallways, through the security checks, and invited him to sit on one side of a long table in a room that was only a little larger than a cubicle. James had to fill out a form describing what he was bringing to his son, but even with the form, a guard outside the cubicle checked James for any weapons (he had already been checked when he entered the facility) and he again checked the bag with Charlie's things.

Another guard brought Charlie into the room, and the first thing that James noticed was that Charlie now had on a blue denim shirt with "Benjamin" embroidered over the pocket, and he had on standard issue brown pants. They sat across from one another for a few seconds in awkward silence until James finally spoke.

"How are you doing, Charlie?"

"Does Heather know?"

"I spoke to Heather yesterday. She knows you are being detained. She doesn't know you've been arrested."

"Did she mention Ryan?"

"Not really. We were mostly talking about the circumstantial evidence and the incident when you pushed your father."

"She told you about that? Why?"

"Your attorney, Henry Moore, wanted to know if there had been any domestic violence in the past."

"That wasn't really domestic violence."

"I believe you. But there is a police report in Winnetka that is still on file. If this goes to trial, the other side will undoubtedly use it against us."

Charlie stared at the floor. He had forgotten about the police report. Of course they would use that against him. He suddenly became more depressed.

"Why can't they find the mechanic?"

"They actually did get into the call history of Jenny's phone, and they have contacted him."

"Why didn't you tell me that when we first sat down? That's great news!"

"Not necessarily. The mechanic is saying that he witnessed an intense argument between you and Jenny. He said that there were obscenities exchanged, and she locked you out of the house."

"That's a complete lie."

"Of course it is, but at this point, it's just his word against yours."

"What about that night?"

"He said that his wife would attest to him being home all night."

"Did Heather say anything else?"

"She said that both she and Ryan love you very much."

"Are you making this up?"

James could see that Charlie's face had completely changed from resignation to a sliver of hope.

"I'm not making it up. It was the last thing she said before we got off the phone."

The guard who had been standing behind the reinforced glass door motioned to James that his time was almost up.

"Don't worry, Charlie. I got us a very astute attorney, and more importantly, you are innocent of any crime."

"I know, but the guy whose cell is across from mine told me that his dad did fifteen years for a murder he didn't commit. It was only DNA testing that finally got him exonerated."

"That's not what is going to happen here. I promise you."

With that, James stood up, handed Charlie a letter and the bag of clothes, and touched his son's hand as he exited the cubicle. It was the last time Charlie would ever see his real father.

As James drove back to Lake Louise, he played out in his head the entire sequence of events leading up to Jenny's disappearance. He kept thinking that there had to be some small detail that had been overlooked, some small clue that would hopefully break open the case.

He arrived home a little after 4:00 P.M. and decided to drive into the village to get an early dinner at the diner. Because of the hour, there were only two men sitting at a table, along with one waitress and the cook, who was also the owner. He decided to sit at the counter, and he had just ordered when one of the men sitting at the table got up and walked over to him.

"You're the man who runs the homeless shelter in Vancouver. Isn't that right?"

"I'm one of the two. As you can see, I'm not doing much there today."

"My brother stayed with you for a week a few years ago. You and your buddy really helped him to get back on his feet."

"That's what we do, give people a hand."

"I think I may know something about your daughter. Your daughter's been missing, right?"

James's heart was racing. This was the break he had been praying for.

"So my buddy over there at the table heard some guy bragging at a bar down in Banff that he'd been getting it every night. His wife can't figure out why he's been so happy."

"May I talk to your friend?"

"He doesn't want to get involved. That's why I came over. You helped my brother. I figured I owed it to you."

"What else do you know?"

"He saw the guy's truck in the parking lot of the bar and he realized that he had called him just a few months earlier when his car had to be towed. While he was riding in the front seat getting his car pulled to Banff, the guy told him about his fishing house on Lake Mead. There are only a few houses down there, and they're only used in the summer."

James remembered that he and Jenny had skied on trails around Lake Mead, but that had probably been five or six years ago. It would take a truck to get to those lake houses this time of year, and James knew that if he contacted the RCMP, they would want search warrants and three days of paperwork before they made a move.

"Thank you for coming over to talk with me. I know that it is often difficult to get involved with other people's business."

"You helped out my family; I wanted to help out yours."

With that the man walked back over and joined his friend at the small table by the window.

James placed fifteen dollars on the counter and got up to leave. He hadn't had a bite to eat, but already he was formulating how he could get to Lake Mead before it got too dark. He thought about going back to the house to get his shotgun, but he remembered the small handgun he kept behind the seat in the pickup. It would have to be enough in case he happened to arrive while the mechanic was there.

Lake Mead was about ten miles southeast of Lake Louise and he guessed correctly that the final five miles would be a rough ride—even for his pickup truck. The sun was just above the mountains to the west, and already the long mountain shadows of the Canadian Rockies were beginning to darken the valleys.

James remembered five or six houses all placed twenty-five or thirty yards apart and only about one hundred feet from the lake. The road next to the lake angled back and forth around the houses so that most of them were hidden from one another. He finally started to get glimpses of the lake through the barren tree branches, and soon he got to the point on the road where he could begin to see several houses up ahead.

The first two houses that he came to were clearly uninhabited, and there were no fresh tire tracks in either of the driveways. The third house was set back a little, but again, no tire tracks in the snow. As he approached the next house, there appeared to be a small lamp burning in one of the windows, and there were tire tracks in the driveway. But before he settled on that as the probable house, he decided to check out the last two houses just to be sure. There was an outside light on above the garage at the last house, but no evidence of any tire tracks.

He turned the truck around and headed back to the house with the lamp in the window.After pulling into the driveway, he retrieved his Glock 38 from behind the seat and checked to be sure that there were the full eight rounds in the chamber. He didn't bother to strap on the holster, but instead grabbed his cowboy hat from the dashboard and concealed the pistol in the top of his hat, which he now carried as he walked to the front door. If he had chosen the wrong house, he wanted it to appear that he was holding his hat as a matter of courtesy, and if there was to be a confrontation, he also wanted to be fully prepared.

He knocked on the door several times. There were no voices and no signs of life. He thought about how there might be other houses around the lake that he didn't know about, and he considered getting back in his truck to continue around the lake road. The snow was at least a foot deep around the exterior of the house, and he only had on his cowboy boots. He checked to see that the safety was set on the Glock, and he carefully placed it in the side pocket of his jacket.He headed around the side of the house and discovered a screened porch that faced the lake. The door that went from the porch into the house appeared to go into the kitchen, and once he had unlatched the outer screen door, he began to knock loudly on the door into the house.

At first he heard nothing, but as he turned to head back out into the snow, he heard a faint whining sound, almost like the sound of a dog that had attempted for the entire day to be disentangled from its leash and had almost given up. James stood dead still on the porch and had to wait almost a minute before he barely heard it again. He tried the door. It wasn't budging a centimeter. He guessed it was probably locked and bolted shut. As he stood there playing with the lock, he heard the faint whining noise a third time.

He took the butt of his gun and broke out one of the panes of glass in the window next to the door. He carefully removed the shards of glass from the broken pane and reached the latch that unlocked the window. Raising the window as high as it would go, he reached in with his right arm and undid the two locks. Entering the kitchen, he began to explore each downstairs room until he came to a locked door, and now he could hear that the sound was coming from that room. Without hesitation, he began to kick at the door with his boots, and while the lock held, he was able to kick a small hole that then became large enough for him to insert his arm. He found the lock and the door swung open.

There was Jenny, tied and gagged to a small daybed and only half covered with a dirty sheet. Her eyes looked vacant. Her hair was matted and off to one side. James gently pulled up the sheet to cover her and he loosened the gag that held her neck and mouth. As soon as the gag was released, she began to cry hysterically and she sounded like a wounded animal. James undid the nylon rope around her wrists and ankles, and once she was free, she curled into a ball.

He held her head in his hands and placed his forehead just above her eyes.

"It's OK, sweetie. I've got you. I've got you, and I'm going to get you out of here. Do you know where he put your clothes?"

"I think they're upstairs."

James darted up the stairs and found Jenny's clothes strewn across a bed. He rushed back down, placed the clothes next to her and headed back into the kitchen to close and lock the door. As he was heading back to check on Jenny, he heard a truck in the driveway.

Jenny was only half dressed, but she had also heard the truck. James looked out the window to the driveway. The truck was intentionally blocking his truck, and a man was getting out of the cab.

"Do you remember how to fire the Glock?"

The two of them had used the gun during target shooting practice just a year ago, so Jenny had some familiarity with how it worked.

"There are eight rounds. Remember to release the safety."

"What are you going to use?"

"We don't want to kill him if we don't have to. I'm going outside to try and talk him down."

"He'll kill you, Papa."

"I don't think so. But he has to believe that you are still locked in the room. Don't fire the Glock unless you hear shots being fired."

"Don't take the risk, Papa. Why don't we just kill him when he walks in the door?"

"Let me try to disarm him without anyone getting killed."

With that, James opened the front door just slightly and yelled out to the man.

"Sir, I just arrived here a few minutes ago. I'm searching for my daughter."

"Your daughter's not here, cowboy. Who told you she was here?"

James opened the door and walked out onto the porch.

"Someone at the diner told me they saw her at Lake Mead."

James noticed that the man was holding a shotgun. It was a Ruger over-under, and if both triggers were pulled simultaneously, it could easily bring down a bear.

"She's not here. I've never seen your daughter, and you're trespassing."

The man kept glancing at the front door as if he half expected Jenny to join her father on the porch.

"Sometimes we make decisions that we later regret, and we think that more bad decisions will solve the problem."

"I don't know anything about your missing daughter, and it's time for you to leave."

"Maybe there is a reason you brought her here, and that reason is not going to go away, even if you make me go away."

"What are you, a psychologist?"

"Nope. I'm just someone who has made his own share of bad decisions. But bad decisions don't have to result in more bad decisions. That's my hope for both of us."

"The only hope for anyone is dumb luck, and once in a while something crosses your path that you can either take and enjoy or leave for the next guy."

"That doesn't sound very satisfying, does it? Just living your life hoping to find the next thing that comes along."

"What is it that you want?"

"I came looking for my daughter; I just want to find her and take her home."

"Right now the only thing is for you to get off of my property."

"I'm happy to do that, but maybe you could put the gun down and move your truck out of the way."

They both just stood there for almost a minute. Finally the man allowed the barrel of his shotgun to drop, and he glanced back at his truck as if he were about to get back in and move it.

James stepped off the porch and began to walk slowly in the direction of the trucks. Just as he thought that the confrontation was over, the mechanic did a sudden snap to, as if he were waking up from a dream. He brought the shotgun up to shoulder level and pulled the trigger. The impact to James's right shoulder knocked him all the way back to the porch, but before he was able to fire the lower chamber, the man's attention was drawn to the sight of Jenny emerging from around the side of the house. She was standing in the snow fully dressed, and her arms were locked in the position James had taught her with the sights of the Glock leveled at the man's head.

Remaining completely motionless, she squeezed the trigger three times and watched as each round tore into his skull. His knees buckled, and his entire body folded like a tent to the ground. She ran over to the porch and saw that her father's right shoulder had been blown away by the impact of the shotgun. There was blood everywhere, but she managed to slide in under him so that his head was resting in her lap.

"Papa, don't try and talk. I'm going to call 911."

"Jenny, don't. They'd never make it out here in time."

"You can't die, Papa. Please don't die."

"You need to help your brother. He's like I was at that age, still searching around for who he is. Charlie needs to get back to Heather and Ryan."

"I'll help him, Papa."

"And Rob will need some help in Vancouver without me there."

"I love you, Papa."

"We made a good little family, Jenny. The two of us made a good little family."

She felt his body go limp, and she saw the life drift out of his eyes. When she was a little girl, he had always tucked her in at night and told her that God's angels were there protecting her. As she held him there under the Alberta sky, she thought of how he had been the one constant in her life, the one source of steady love that had always gotten her through.

In his cell in Edmonton, Charlie opened the letter that his father had given him just a few hours earlier.

Dear Charlie,

I just want you to know how proud I am to have you as my son. We've only known each other for a short while, but already I can see myself in you—or at least the way I was at your age.

Pretty soon you'll see that the most important thing is to take really good care of those around you—Heather and Ryan to be sure, but also anyone you meet—even if it is only for five minutes. Look for opportunities to be kind, and you will come to find that your heart will be full of a joy that will sustain you, no matter the circumstances.

I know that it is really difficult being in prison and separated from your family, but find people there who you can support and care for. That will make your days in prison go much more quickly!

We all love you, and look forward to the day when we come to bring you home.

Love,
Dad

Charlie read the letter three times and fell asleep. He couldn't help but feel that his father was there with him in prison, and he had the distinct feeling that all would be well.

CHAPTER NINETEEN

BETWEEN SEPTEMBER AND DECEMBER, I TOOK ADDITIONAL "baby steps," attempting to put the needs of fellow prisoners above my own. I knew that by that point, my job at the Bank was long gone, and that Melissa had probably forgotten about me in favor of Gerard Hugel or perhaps David Fortran. I still hoped to run into Jonathan at Arthur Road, but with thousands of incarcerated prisoners, it seemed unlikely—especially since I had no idea what he looked like.

I had my state-appointed attorney contact both Jenny and Catherine. I was hoping that Catherine could somehow find some funding for Jenny's tuition, and I wanted Jenny to know that I was in prison in Bombay. I knew that she would forgive me for whatever problems I had caused her at NYU, and I didn't want her to worry about me, although I knew she would be distraught to hear the news.

Despite my newly discovered ability to help and care for other people, I still experienced moments of complete despair. My attorney seemed confused about my motivation to bribe a judge, and he was candid about the devastating evidence of the tape recording if my case ever came to trial. In short, I couldn't imagine any scenario that might bring about my release from Arthur Road, and in that despair I began to talk to God.

Instead of asking for a litany of things I wanted God to do for me, I asked him to help me understand that despite my incarceration, I was still a human being with the capacity to love. I wanted to know how a fuller appreciation of my humanity might result in renewed purpose and clarity for my life.

At the small Christmas service that was held in the same holding tank I had stayed in on my arrival, I finally surrendered all of my life to God and Christ. Each of us were given a small candle at the end of that service, and in the weeks and months that followed, I held that candle in my right hand whenever I prayed.

I received one card for Christmas that year, and it was from Jenny. The address on the outside simply said:

JAMES MONROE
ARTHUR ROAD JAIL
BOMBAY, INDIA

It was loaded with international stamps, and it had a smiley face across the flap on the other side. On the front of the card were angels coming down from heaven announcing the birth of Jesus, and she had signed it, "Always your loving daughter, Jenny."

The message on the other side of the card was something I will always treasure.

"Dear Papa,

Wanted you to know that I got mostly A's this term at NYU! Sorry to hear about prison. I have your picture next to my bed, and I look at it every day. It reminds me of what a good person you are. I also know that you didn't hurt anyone. My hope is that we will all be back together soon.

Don't worry about the tuition. Mom and I got it all worked out. I will love you forever!

Love, Jenny."

It was the card that kept me going into the New Year, and it was my hope for reunion with Jenny that made each day at Arthur Road something I could bear.

Around the middle of January I noticed that Ramesh had stopped eating and a few evenings later he was slumped over against the wall. I managed to work my way next to him and I allowed his head to rest on my shoulder. He had congestion and a deep cough that suggested pneumonia or something equally virulent. He had a temperature and his tongue was swollen in his mouth, making it almost impossible for him to talk. Without money for the wardens, medical care was only a remote possibility, so when I requested aspirin from one of them, I was fully expecting a shrug and a nod of the head, which meant "no." Instead he reappeared about thirty minutes later with a full bottle of baby aspirin, and I carefully fed five or six of them to Ramesh. As a result he slept through the night, and the same warden allowed both of us to miss work detail so that Ramesh could continue to recover. There are small pockets of compassion in prison, and they often surface just at the point of unrelenting despair. It took Ramesh almost ten days to recover, and the evenings I spent comforting him continue to be the touchstone I return to when I question my ability to put others' needs above my own.

Other inmates were not as fortunate as Ramesh, and every morning two or three deceased inmates were removed from the barracks on stretchers as the pestilence gained momentum. The wardens wanted to avoid touching anything related to death, and they wore surgical masks everywhere except for their own quarters. Healthy inmates were employed to dispose of clothing and bedding, and one morning I was sent to the laundry with a canvas bag full of infected blankets.

The prison laundry is in the basement, and to get there I had to pass by the room where I was tortured several months before. I now considered that room a sacred space—a place where all hope was lost, and in the complete absence of light, a newness emerged like a nascent star.

Two wardens stopped me along the way to ask where I was going. As soon as they saw the blankets, they turned the other way and let me pass. When I arrived at the laundry window, the inmate in charge had his back to me. He was preoccupied with rearranging a rack of wardens' uniforms.

"How can I help you mate?"

It was the first Australian accent I had heard since arriving at Arthur Road.

"These are contaminated blankets. The warden sent me down to get them laundered."

"It's a nasty infection going around. You ought to wash your hands. How about a sink?"

At that, the young Aussie opened the half door and invited me into the laundry. Huge machines lined both walls, and I wondered why all the equipment was needed for a prison that never washed any of the inmates' clothing or bedding.

"How long you been in the Road?"

"About eight months, and you?"

"Going on three and a half years."

"You wouldn't know a fellow Aussie by the name of Jonathan Samuel?"

He looked at me as if I had just told him that he was being released. Instead of surprise, he gazed at me with an intense interest.

"I am Jonathan Samuel."

I had given up on the idea of ever meeting Jonathan, and for a moment I too was speechless.

"I know your sister. You are the reason I came to Bombay!"

Jonathan looked around as if I had just revealed an escape plan, and he immediately lowered his voice to a whisper.

"How in bloody hell did you end up in here?"

As he spoke we moved toward the back of the laundry. Normally a patrol of wardens would be checking the laundry on a regular basis, but because of the spreading pestilence it was perceived as a place of even more deadly infection. And normally I would have been missed if I hadn't returned to the barracks, but the wardens were spending limited contact time with the prisoners in hopes of increasing their own chances for survival. I knew that in these circumstances, I could create an alibi for my absence.

As I told him about my relationship with Melissa and the failed plan to bribe the judge, he looked at me knowingly, almost as if he had heard it all before. There were several times when he started to interrupt me and then paused, wanting me to complete my story, which was now sounding somewhat similar to his own. As he began his own story of arriving in Bombay and his arrest for smuggling drugs, I noticed that there was an insistence about him that reminded me of Melissa. Physically, he had the same high cheekbones and prominent forehead. Prison eventually diminishes an inmate's physical vitality, but in Jonathan's case, flickers of his former self were still intact.

"Melissa was in love with the French ambassador to Australia. Before he met her, he had an affair with another employee of the embassy. Her irate ex-husband was threatening to go to The Sydney Morning Herald with the story, and he wanted $100,000 US to keep quiet. Melissa knew that some of my mates had scored five times that in drug runs into Bombay. They had been running drugs for years, and they never got caught. She didn't make me do the run, but she knew that she would lose the ambassador if the story ever went to press. I wanted to do it for her.

Twelve hours before I left for Bombay, my connection here was arrested. In a plea deal, he revealed the drop off points and the timetable. Like you, I walked into a trap, and two days later, I was incarcerated at Arthur Road. When they allowed me to call Melbourne fourteen months ago, Melissa wasn't there, but I told my mother to tell Melissa that the only possible way out is to bribe a judge. I guess that's where you came in."

This immediately confirmed my latent suspicion that I had been Melissa's "mark" since the day we first met at Victoria Falls. Perhaps for her, our relationship had been a slow build until she sensed that the opportunity was there to ask me to go to Bombay. For all I knew, she had invented the plan sitting in my room at The Victoria Falls Hotel, and all of the flirtation and innuendo were a way to bring me along. I attempted to process all of this as I sat across from Jonathan, and he must have noticed my distraction as well as my chagrin.

"As you undoubtedly know, Melissa is somewhat of an enigma. When we were younger, she always stood up for me as her younger brother. She was the person I could go to when my life was in turmoil. Our father left when I was four and she was seven. A part of me believes that her entire life has been spent searching for his replacement. She has always dated older men, and her fear of separation means that she has a hard time committing to anyone. Most men regard her as aloof and unattainable, but she has a sweet and vulnerable side that she only reveals when she begins to let down her guard."

The animosity and suspicion that I had assumed about her only a moment ago now turned to understanding or even sympathy. Of course I had been the father figure in our relationship. I was the one who had made all the arrangements for travel and accommodation. I had waited like a patient parent as she tried on dresses; I had even interceded on her behalf with Gerard Hugel. Her comment about ending it if it didn't "feel right" were her caution lights coming on. Would I walk out of her life like her father did? Maybe her cautionary statement was a preemptive strike in case I did decide to leave.

But it wasn't just her fear of separation that haunted her. It was her awareness that she had a spirituality about her that had undoubtedly been present since childhood. It gave her an intensity that was both charismatic and charming, much like an ancient goddess who could transform herself at will into a beautiful swan. I had voluntarily become captive, even obeisant to her charm, but there was a capriciousness about it that later became off-putting and, in retrospect, a little foolish. For Melissa, it was an elusive echo of her innermost being that was eternally fascinating and yet morally inconsequential. Part of its attraction for me was the elusiveness of what it promised to be: the answer to my longing for sacred meaning and purpose outside of myself. What I had learned in prison is that the path to that meaning and purpose is not one of endless fascination, but rather one of unconditional love for those around us.

Our conversation had only lasted ten minutes when a warden came to the window wanting to pick up his laundry. I hid behind a dryer, and as soon as Jonathan returned, I embraced him as a comrade. We were both essentially in the same boat. Melissa was our common hope of somehow getting out of Arthur Road. We both loved her in our own ways, but her capricious nature did not bode well for a plan of escape. While I embraced him, I silently forgave her for our plight. She may have conveniently forgotten about both of us, but to live on that assumption would only embitter what would undoubtedly be an extended travail of incarceration.

The next month was the most difficult month I spent at Arthur Road. The wardens refused to separate the men who became ill, and as a result, the large room where we were housed was infested with disease. Coughing became an incessant cacophony, and as more inmates passed away, there was a fear of infection that caused the healthy inmates to claim certain spaces as safety zones. Sick inmates were relegated to the end of the room closest to the latrine, and even the wardens kept their distance. The several times that I ventured into the area of sickness to try and offer a blanket or fresh water, Ramesh pulled me back, pleading with me to stay away. It became a test of my newly acquired faith. In the end, when the illness began to subside, I felt guilty that I had not done enough for those who had suffered and died.

Around noon on a Tuesday in late February, I was called into the superintendent's office and told that I should come back the next morning to meet with someone called Mr. Alexis. I suspected that Mr. Alexis was probably the new state-appointed attorney, since my attorney had indicated at our last meeting that he was being taken off the case. One of the wardens came for me around 10:00 A.M. the next morning and told me to bring all of my things. I only had a plastic bag of personal items, but I brought it with me, thinking that maybe I was being moved to one of the other barracks.

When I walked into the superintendent's office, there was an American sitting there in a three-piece suit. The superintendent introduced him to me as Daniel Alexis.

"Are you James Monroe?"

"I am."

"I'm here representing a third party who has secured your release."

At first I couldn't speak. I thought maybe it was part of some cruel joke that the prison played on inmates who were getting too comfortable.

"Mr. Alexis has also procured an expedited release, so you'll be leaving Arthur Road before the end of the day."

My mind was racing. Who could have procured my release? Earlier in my life I might have grabbed my things and made a quick exit, but I wanted to at least attempt to procure a release for Ramesh and Jonathan. I knew that at least Ramesh would do the same for me.

"I'd like to request that two other inmates—Ramesh Jariwala and Jonathan Samuel—be released as well."

This was a request that neither Mr. Alexis nor the superintendent were expecting, and they looked at one another, somewhat bewildered. I was taken back to my barracks and I didn't hear anything until a little after 3:00 P.M. I was suspecting that my request had also jeopardized my own release, so I was relieved when I again saw Mr. Alexis sitting in the office.

"You may choose one of your fellow inmates to be released, but not both. We'll give you an hour to decide."

I was returned to the barracks. I had less than forty-five minutes to decide between Ramesh and Jonathan. I knew that there was a possibility that Melissa had arranged my release, but if she had the wherewithal to do so, why would she have chosen me over Jonathan? There was a slight possibility that the Bank had procured my freedom, but they would not want the potential press release that one of their own had attempted to bribe an Indian judge, and they certainly would not consider paying for an additional prisoner to be released.

I thought of Ramesh, still faithfully wearing his Yankees hat several years from now and still incarcerated. Who would care for him when he again became sick? Who would regale him with stories about New York? At the same time I realized that if I chose Jonathan I would be able to complete my original mission to Bombay. There was a chance that Melissa was still unattached in Nairobi, and my return with a freed Jonathan would have the same effect I had envisioned months before. There was at least a possibility that I could be reinstated at the Bank and return to the life I had left behind. I thought of Melissa welcoming me with open arms and the nights we would spend together upon my return to Nairobi. For a moment, all the intoxication, all the physicality of her came rushing back, and I couldn't imagine not choosing Jonathan. It was at that moment that one of the wardens came to get me, and as I walked to the superintendent's office, I was still uncertain who I would choose.

When I arrived, both the superintendent and Mr. Alexis were standing, and there was a formality in the room that had not been there earlier. It was clear that they wanted to get on with it.

"We need your decision."

I looked around the room. Through the superintendent's window, I could see the prison yard, and beyond that, the street where I had arrived ten months ago. I knew that in a matter of minutes I would be out of prison forever. I would return to freedom; they needed my answer.

"I choose Ramesh Jariwala."

The superintendent and Mr. Alexis looked at one another, and then the superintendent directed the warden to bring Ramesh to the office.

When he walked into the office a few minutes later, the superintendent said something to Ramesh in Hindi. Whatever the superintendent said to him produced a large smile. For a moment, the four of us just stood there as if no one knew quite what to do. Ramesh was accompanied back to the barracks to gather his few belongings. The two of us then signed several release forms, and Mr. Alexis, Ramesh, and I were escorted to the entrance by one of the wardens.

It was an early spring day in Bombay, warm but with low humidity. There was a crowd outside the entrance, similar to the day when I first arrived. Because of the bright sunshine, both Ramesh and I shielded our eyes for a moment to allow them to adjust, and as I gazed beyond the crowd and across the street, there was Teresa Benjamin standing next to a car with an infant in her arms.

Of course she was impeccably dressed, and as our eyes met, she gave me a wave as if we had just seen each other yesterday. Teresa Benjamin had come to Bombay to rescue me from prison! She was delivering on the promise she had made during my departure at Victoria Falls. I grabbed Ramesh's hand and pulled him with me through the crowd.

I hadn't kissed a woman in almost a year, but I kissed Teresa several times as we embraced. As we put our heads together, I whispered "thank you" several times into her ear.

Ramesh was completely amazed. I hadn't mentioned any

woman to him, and now he was out of prison and seeing me embrace a beautiful American woman. I introduced Ramesh to Teresa, and they started to shake hands, but then also embraced.

"I've brought you a little surprise, James. This is Charlie Benjamin, but his last name should really be Monroe. He's our baby!"

The baby in her arms now looked up and gave me a smile. Teresa had come to Bombay to get me out of prison and to bring me our baby!

She handed him to me and I carefully shielded his eyes from the sun.

"He's beautiful, Teresa. He's beautiful and handsome all at the same time."

Teresa, Charlie, Ramesh, and I all piled into the back of the town car Teresa had hired to make the trip across town. I then heard Teresa say to the driver, "Taj Hotel."

"You're looking a little haggard, James. I bought you some clothes, but you look like you could also use a cocktail."

Ramesh and I were still in our prison clothes, and we must have appeared to our driver as a strange juxtaposition: two convicts, a stylish American woman and a baby. We represented a backstory that he could not have begun to imagine. He must have been equally amazed when we asked him to take a detour to Ramesh's neighborhood, and we all watched his mother's reaction when he suddenly appeared at her front door. As he and his mother embraced, he paused and gave me a quick glance of gratitude. In just six months I had come to think of him as my son. Teresa squeezed my hand as we headed for the hotel. I kept thinking I was still in prison, and this was only a late night dream. But now we were returning to the exact spot where my nightmare in Bombay had begun.

As we boarded the elevator it occurred to me that it was the same elevator I had taken ten months ago for my fateful meeting with the Indian judge. Now I was looking forward to a hot shower and dinner with Teresa and Charlie. I was elated to find that my passport was still in the hotel safe along with my wallet. I wouldn't be needing my World Bank credentials, but they were there as well.

After showering, I collapsed on the bed and awakened to find that it was already early evening. Instead of going immediately to meet Teresa, I decided to take a walk in the direction of the water, and so I headed over to the Gateway of India, built in the 1920s to commemorate British sovereignty in the region and an earlier visit to India by King George V.

The sun was setting on the Arabian Sea and beyond that the Indian Ocean stretched all the way to Africa. I would probably never return to Zimbabwe or Kenya, and yet I thought of the day I had first met Teresa at Victoria Falls. Little did I know that our brief interlude would form the basis of life's promise for decades to come.

I had grown up believing that some moments, some places are where the sacred lies, and that others—even everything else—is a reality left untouched by the face of God. But that perception is a lie. It all is sacred; it all is holy: a woman's exquisite beauty, the pain of loss, the despair of incarceration are all sanctified parts of life that are forever intertwined. The mighty Zambezi will continue to be flung headlong into the gorge of Victoria Falls. The mist of rainbows will continue to rise. Our children will continue as our final legacy of what we had hoped life would be.

EPILOGUE

AS I FELL BACK ASLEEP, I SAW MYSELF STANDING UNDER the same boughs of snow-filled pine at the edge of Lake Moraine. As the snow continued to fall, I stood there in the complete quiet, allowing the snow to settle on my face and hands until I became numb and completely immobilized. Still standing in my skis, I began to dream of dying, of drifting into oblivion. The cold, the tall pines, the distant view of the lake made the idea irresistible. They would find me days later, still preserved by the cold and the snow, having returned to the natural world in a remote section of western Canada. I was almost there when I heard a voice calling my name way up the trail. As the figure drew closer, I recognized my father. He looked much younger, like the pictures I had seen of him when he was in Africa.

He greeted me by saying my name, and as he drew closer, he gave me a broad smile. Instead of continuing to speak, he began to brush away the snow from my face and hands. As he did so, the cold and numbness began to subside and feeling returned to my limbs. He did this several times, much in the way a sculptor would put the finishing touches on a statue. He was incredibly precise, even brushing away snow that had accumulated in my collar and around my eyes. As he brought me back to life I wanted to thank him, but I was still unable to speak. It was as if the cold had permeated my throat and lungs, so that I was now mobile but still without a voice.

Satisfied that I was ready for the journey home, he glided back onto the trail and made a motion for me to follow. I was able to perfectly mimic the strides of his forward progress, and soon I was matching him in both speed and technique as we effortlessly traversed towards the trailhead. As we neared the clearing that leads up to the house, I saw Jenny standing in the driveway. She was smiling, and she waved to both of us as we drew closer. I looked to my left, but now my father was gone. He had evaporated in midstride. Finding my voice, I shouted to Jenny.

"I've been with Father. He found me on the trail."

At that moment, I was awakened by another voice; it was the guard's voice on the other side of the prison bars.

"Pipe down in there. You're calling for your father, but he's no longer here. He left hours ago."

I was startled and disoriented. I had been talking in my sleep. I suddenly realized that no one was there—not James, not Jenny, not even Teresa. I couldn't blame the mishaps of my life on Richard or Heather or anyone else. Whatever I had done or not done up to that point could only be resolved by my own resilience, my own determination. I remembered what James had said about the importance of every interaction with humanity, of finding life in every moment.

As I lay there trembling, I wondered if the appearance of Jenny in my dream meant that she had somehow been found. I knew that her reappearance was the last chance I had of being exonerated, but I didn't want to live on that hope if she was gone forever, or worse, if she was now dead. For all we knew, the mechanic had taken her to another Canadian province or even sold her in

Vancouver. I couldn't imagine the degradation she might be experiencing at this very moment, so I attempted to put it out of my mind. So much negative apprehension was swirling in my psyche that I was unable to bring clarity to any part of it.

After breakfast that morning, I was summoned to the superintendent's office. I thought I was going to be moved to yet another Canadian prison. Perhaps they were anticipating that I would be accused of murder, and they planned to move me to a maximum security facility. Whatever it was, they took me to a small anteroom and told me to wait.

After about thirty minutes, a guard appeared with a clipboard and several papers covered in small print. My glasses were back in my cell, but I assumed that the release forms I signed were a formality whenever a prisoner is moved from one facility to another. After signing, I waited for an hour, until another guard appeared with my civilian clothes. He went with me to my cell where I changed and gathered my things. I carefully placed the letter from James in my right pocket, and other inmates watched as I was led away.

Outside there was an RCMP sedan waiting in the driveway and my handcuffs were removed as they motioned for me to sit in the rear seat. About twenty miles from the prison, I noticed that we were heading north. I assumed that I was being taken to a larger prison in Calgary, but even with the little I knew about Canadian geography, we seemed to be headed in the wrong direction. Soon some of the landmarks became more familiar, and I suddenly realized that we were headed toward Lake Louise. For reasons that I could not begin to fathom, it appeared that they were taking me back to Jenny's.

When we pulled into the driveway, Jenny's car was there, along with James's truck. It had started to snow, and both cars were lightly covered in white. There was another RCMP sedan as well, and next to the sedan, Inspector Macpherson was standing, watching us pull up the drive. As our car pulled up next to his and he reached over to open my door, I climbed out, and both of us just stood there looking at each other. I could tell that he was about to offer some sort of explanation, but whatever he had rehearsed had suddenly escaped him. It was the first time I had noticed any awkwardness in his otherwise unflappable demeanor.

"Charlie, quite a bit has happened in the past eighteen hours."

It was the first time he had ever addressed me by my first name, and I quickly jumped to the conclusion that they had found Jenny and she was dead.

"We went down the wrong rabbit hole on this one, and I apologize that you so quickly became our chief suspect. Obviously we got it all wrong."

I looked beyond him and into the windows of the house. It was mostly dark and the falling snow had begun to cover it like a shroud.

"Is Jenny dead?"

Macpherson paused, allowing the weight of what he was about to say to settle into my late morning arrival.

"Jenny isn't dead. In fact she is inside waiting. She has some very unfortunate news to share with you."

I glanced over at James's truck. His cowboy hat was missing from the dash, and now the unthinkable came crashing in. I walked slowly towards the house. Even before I reached the front door, I knew that James was dead, that he had died in some tragic encounter as he had attempted to save Jenny. I pushed the door open and looked across the hallway and into the darkened stairwell. There was Jenny sitting halfway up the stairs, her face red and swollen, her hair knotted and off to one side. She had on sweatpants and a sweater that was too big for her. It must have belonged to James. For the first time we looked at each other as brother and sister.

I walked up and sat next to her. As I put my arm around her, she began to shudder and weep.

"This is all my fault, Charlie. I should have been more careful how I dressed around that monster. Papa would still be alive. It's my fault that Papa had to die."

"It isn't anyone's fault, Jenny. What happened isn't anyone's fault. Our father died doing what he did best."

We sat there like that well into the afternoon as it continued to snow. By not moving, we both wanted to stop time, to retreat back into the past, to stall James's full departure. Finally, I made tea and we sat in front of the fire. Jenny told me everything that had happened. When she got to the part about cradling James in her lap as he passed away, each phrase was interrupted by a sob from the back of her throat. That moment helped me to understand fully the depth of their relationship—father, mentor, confidante, and friend. I envied her for all the years they had spent together, and I realized that my relationship with Richard had been a charade of what is supposed to occur between a parent and a child. Suddenly, I wanted to talk to Heather and Ryan. Whatever fantasy I had been chasing by coming to Alberta had been replaced by a new fervor to make things right for my own family.

"Hello?" Heather's voice sounded distant and exhausted.

"I'm out of prison."

Neither of us spoke for about thirty seconds.

"Charlie, what happened?"

"My father found Jenny, but he was killed trying to free her."

Heather again paused before responding.

"Oh my God, Charlie. I am so sorry. What an ordeal."

"The funeral is this weekend in Vancouver, but I'm not going."

"After all of this, don't you need to be there?"

"My father would understand. He would want me to be with you and Ryan."

"What about your sister? Doesn't she need you there for support?"

"My father's friend, Rob Curtin, is arriving here tomorrow morning. He and Jenny will return to Vancouver together. He will be with her at the funeral."

"Ryan wants to say hello."

"Are you coming home, Dad?"

"Ryan, I love you, and I'm coming home."

"I've missed you, Dad, and I love you too."

As Ryan handed the phone back to Heather, I wanted my goodbye to be as reassuring as possible.

"Heather, I know that talk is cheap, but this time I am coming home for good."

Heather's voice was flat, but there was a thread of hope in her goodbye.

"Drive safely, Charlie. It will be good to see you."

After dinner that evening, Jenny showed me several pictures that she had found in James's wallet. The first was one of the two of them downhill skiing somewhere in western Canada. They both looked happy and fully alive. The second was a much younger Teresa holding an infant.

"The background looks like Africa."

"Or India. Your mother is wearing a sari with a sash. It may well be the same sash that hangs above Papa's desk in his bedroom. This third picture is a young man from India, probably in his early twenties. He has on a Yankees baseball cap and the woman he is standing next to is probably his mother. Whoever he is, he was important enough to Papa that he carried his picture."

Before going up to James's room to spend my last night in Alberta, I wandered outside, just as I had done the first night I arrived in Lake Louise. The snow had finally blown off to the east and the sky was a cascade of brilliant starlight. I wondered about my father and his brief time with my mother in Africa. Both of them were now dead, and whatever secrets they had together were forever sealed. I thought of my father, just a few years older than I, deep in the African continent and under the night sky. How even at middle age he still had his whole life before him, much as I have mine.

Entering his bedroom, I saw that Jenny had placed his cowboy hat on a small hook next to the door. As I looked around the room, I again wondered how much any of us can know about another person's life. There may be pictures or even diaries, but all the vagaries of a person's existence are forever a mystery once they are gone.

From talking to Jenny and from spending a few days with him, I knew that he had been married and divorced. I knew that he had slept with my mother in Africa. But at some point the pursuit of women had been replaced by a stronger allegiance. I wondered what had been the catalyst for that change. I guessed that it was prison, but it was unlikely that incarceration alone would produce such a transformation.

What was obvious to me was that my father was a private person and within that privacy there existed an insatiable curiosity for life's meaning. That pursuit eventually eclipsed everything else—his career, his relationships with women, and even the insecurities that had plagued him as a young man. He was insistent on exploring matters of the heart, the elements of compassion, no matter how unconventional or outrageous that journey might become. The constant striving for fame or advantage that had once dominated him had been supplanted by a quiet confidence. It took courage to pursue that path, and once there, he undoubtedly discovered the presence of God.

At some point in his life my father had stopped feeling the need to explain himself—either to others or, more importantly, to himself. Without the burden of always feeling that he needed to justify his life to others, he was free to be a man without pretense. It was that freedom that he had spent a lifetime bestowing to Jenny, and that he had now in only a matter of days bestowed to me.

CPSIA information can be obtained
at www.ICGtesting.com
Printed in the USA
LVHW021308071218
599551LV00004B/5/P